Enough

J. Asmara

Facebook: www.facebook.com/authorjasmara

Instagram: @AuthorJAsmara

Email: theasmara@yahoo.com

Twitter: @AuthorJAsmara

This novel is a work of fiction. Any resemblances to actual events, real people, living or dead, organizations, establishments or locales are products of the author's imagination. Other names, characters, places, and incidents are used fictitiously.

SPECIAL THANKS

To my cover models Juliette Howard,
Liza Biggs, and Patrick Howard. Thank you for helping
bring my vision to life. You all are amazing. To my
cover designer Michael Horne it's always a pleasure to
work with you. You are a talented man who does wonderful
work. To my beta readers Rene Holmes and Tonya Edwards
thanks for your time and patience with me. Finally to my lil
"Big Pig" Khyli Adams. Thanks for the name for the story.
Teedy loves you baby girl!

ACKNOWLEDGMENTS

I want to thank everyone who said or did anything supportive during my process. I really appreciate you all. There have been several special people that I would like to take this time to personally acknowledge.

First and foremost I want to thank God for blessing me with the strength and ability to accomplish this. My faith in Him is what started my writing journey. Faith is the substance of things hoped for, the evidence of things not seen. Thank you Lord.

Secondly, I want to thank my family and friends. To my parents Mikell and Lillian thank you for all of your support. I am where I am because of the both of you. To my children Jay'Quan, Jessica, and Jaden you all are my motivation. Everything I do is for you guys. To my friends Angela, Chenika, Karene, and Robinne you all are truly the definition of friends. I would not be here without you guys. You all have played very important roles in my growth as an author. Thank you for not letting me quit. I love you ladies.

Last but certainly not least, I want to thank all of my readers. Thank you for your support. I am very proud of what I've done and I hope you enjoy what I created for you.

Much love,

J. Asmara

Contents

CHAPTER 1
Jamya "Mya" Adams

At five foot eight with a small waist and juicy booty, Jamya "Mya" Adams was a hundred and forty pound beauty that was not to be pushed around. Growing up in the projects she'd fought her whole life and never backed down from anyone. Jamya was raised in the streets of south side Chicago in a single parent household. She watched her mother Cynthia struggle to provide for her and her two little sisters Jasmine and Jessie. Because of that Jamya started hustling when she was twelve years old.

Jamya's partner in crime was her best friend Jalyssa Perez. Jalyssa was a spicy Puerto Rican that was not scared of anything. They started with breaking into houses for items to pawn, and then graduated to selling marijuana throughout their high school years. Jamya and Jalyssa were on a roll in their dabbling in crime until they were picked up by an undercover police officer while peddling their weed on the corner. Luckily they only had a few nickel bags left between the two of them at the time so the girls got a slap on the wrist with community service. That was their wakeup call that the streets were watching them and they realized that they had haters.

Jamya and Jalyssa were at Jamya's house watching *Player's Club* when the quote "use what you got to get what you want" jumped out at Jamya.

"That's what we got to do Lyssa."

"What the hell are you talking about Mya? I know I'm fine and all," Jalyssa said as she caressed her five foot six bodacious body, "but I ain't up for no stripping."

"No, not stripping," Jamya said as she moved her hand to her chin in thought.

"Oh hell. What you up to in that brain of yours?"

"Alright check this. We had to chill on our weed game. We're cool now but the little coins we got saved up won't last. We're too grown now to be hitting houses like we did back in the day."

"Okay."

"We're finer than a motherfucker so let's use that. I'm thinking we start hitting these dumb fuckers that be all in our faces. Straight jack they shit. They'd never know what happened."

"Girl you're crazy, but you know I'm down with you mama. Let's do it."

Jamya smiled, "Cool I think I have a plan."

Jamya plotted and planned until she devised an outline for their new hustle. Her mastermind plan had them in and out of town running scams on numerous unsuspecting men. Though the girls loved the streets, they were smart enough to know that they needed an education. They graduated high school and then attended a local community college. Over the course of their two years at Olive-Harvey Community College Jamya and Jalyssa made enough money to move their families out of the projects.

"Jamya I don't know what you're into and you're too stubborn and secretive to tell me what you have going on. Just be careful baby girl," Cynthia said when Jamya brought home the keys to their new apartment.

"Chill Ma. I'm going to be alright. You just worry about getting you, Jasmine, and Jessie settled in. The rent's paid up for six months and the train isn't far from the apartment."

"Thank you baby girl," she said through tears.

Jamya got her family straight while Jalyssa was two floors down doing the same for her mom and little brother.

Life changed drastically for Jamya and Jalyssa six months after moving their mothers out of the projects. They graduated college; Jamya with her degree in Business Management and Jalyssa with her degree in Web Design. They decided to go out and celebrate on graduation night.

While at a local club they found a mark in a flossed out, spending money to show I got it type of guy.

"I know we're supposed to be here celebrating but he's an easy target," Jalyssa said.

"I don't know Lyssa. I kind of want to chill tonight."

"Mya we can chill anytime. Look at that watch, those earrings, and shit look at them shoes. He got money."

Jamya analyzed the guy and realized Jalyssa was right. "Okay Lyssa. Let's do this."

The girls baited the guy by dancing seductively his way. Once they got his attention they began touching each other periodically. That quickly woke up his desire to have them both.

"Hello ladies," he said over the loud music. "I'm Chris."

"I'm April and this is my girl Elaina," Jamya said with an emphasis on "girl".

Chris totally ate up the sexual aura the girls put out. "Y'all are the finest ladies in this place for real."

"Bet you've told all the ladies up in here the same thing," Jalyssa said with her sassiness.

Chris smiled, "Nah shorty. I'm for real. I'm in town just for the night and I'd love to holla at y'all ladies, get some drinks, and maybe chill afterwards."

Chris was happier than a fly on shit when they said yes. He

perpetrated to be all hard and the man in the streets but in actuality he was just a two bit street hustler that had stolen a large amount of money from a not too happy group of people; which was his main reason for only being in town for that night.

After several drinks and meaningless conversation Jamya, Jalyssa, and Chris left the club. They ended up at the Best Motel off the interstate. Jamya and Jalyssa sat in the old school Caprice while Chris went to the trunk and then went to the hotel's check in window to get the room. Jamya wondered what he got out of the trunk hoping it wasn't a gun because she didn't have hers on her.

"Y'all honeys ready?" Chris asked when he returned to the car.

"Yeah, let's go have some fun," Jamya said.

They got into the simple room and Chris said, "Let's get this party started."

"Okay papi but first take one of these," Jalyssa said taking an ecstasy pill out of her purse.

"What the fuck is that?"Chris said to Jalyssa.

"Just a little X to pump this party up. It'll be a night you won't forget," Jalyssa replied.

"I don't-"

"Uh uh uh. You're only in town for tonight. Let's make it

an amazing night," Jamya said as she put the pill to his lips. Chris obeyed and took the pill. "Now swallow," she paused as he swallowed. "Good boy," she said with a peck on the lips.

Jalyssa came with some water from the bathroom. "Drink this."

"Now, let's get this party started," Jamya said as she stripped down to her bra and panties.

"Hell yeah! You fine as hell shorty."

"Thank you," Jamya said with a sneaky grin. She knew it wouldn't be long before the X kicked in and he'd be ready to fuck so she pranced around the room teasing him until that happened. The plan then was that they'd fuck his brains out until he passed out. While he laid there with his thumb in his mouth they'd take his shit and bounce. It always worked like clockwork.

Jamya saw the affects of the ecstasy kicking in and knew it was time. "Take your clothes off and lay down on the bed," she instructed.

Once Chris undressed and laid down Jalyssa took over. She was a pro at dick sucking and she'd have any man ready to bust in minutes. Jamya let him play with her tits as Jalyssa sucked him off. It started to feel real good to him and he said, "Oh shit. Hold on shorty, I'm about to nut. Oh shit. I'm about to…"

Chris didn't get a chance to finish his sentence because he started convulsing. Jalyssa jerked her head back and she and Jamya both stood there with their eyes bulged out.

"What the fuck?" Jalyssa said.

"Oh shit," Jamya replied as she grabbed Jalyssa's arm. She knew they'd fucked up. Chris started foaming at the mouth and then the convulsing stopped.

"Oh shit Mya. Is he dead?" Jalyssa asked with her hand flying to her chest.

Jamya slowly moved to Chris and checked his pulse. She shifted her hands around his wrist several times before she said, "Fuck! He's dead Lyssa."

Jalyssa started speaking in Spanish as she paced back and forth. "Calm down Jalyssa. You know I don't be understanding that shit when you get upset."

"I can't go to jail Mya. Fuck. We're not made for that shit."

"Chill. We're not going to jail. Let me think."

Jalyssa continued to pace as Jamya came up with a plan to get them out of the situation. "Okay I got it," Jamya said as she started putting her clothes back on.

"Go get a rag with some hot water and soap on it. And then-"

"What the fuck?"

"Just listen. Get it and then wipe his dick to get your salvia and any other DNA off his shit."

"Oh…Okay. Good thinking."

"Once you get it nice and soapy. Turn the water off and wipe the knob with the rag. Go ahead and get that. I'm about to go through his pockets. Then we need to take that cup you used for water and wipe it along with as much else as we can down."

"I knew all that CSI bullshit you be watching would come in handy one day," Jalyssa said laughing.

"Whatever. Make sure you don't touch too much."

Jalyssa went to the bathroom and Jamya grabbed her "hoe" pouch out of her purse. That was where she kept things like extra underwear, condoms, vaginal wipes, lubricants and such, and miscellaneous survival items. Jamya pulled out a set of rubber gloves and some hand sanitizer. Jalyssa didn't know just how far Jamya's obsession with crime scene shows was. She put on one of the gloves and went into Chris' pocket. She found a money clip with fifteen hundred dollars, receipts, a condom, and his car keys.

Jalyssa came back into the room. "Find anything good?"

"Fifteen Gs."

"That's what's up. Seven fifty isn't bad."

"Yeah but we're not taking it all."

"Fuck you mean Mya?"

"We're going to leave three hundred in the clip. Trust me Lyssa. You got your burner phone on you?"

"Yeah. Why?"

"Once we clear out of here we're going to call the police."

"Oh shit Mya!"

"Listen Jalyssa. This motherfucker is dead! This goes beyond getting picked up for robbing a motherfucker. We don't know if anyone saw us or if this piece of shit motel has cameras. So by calling the police as some party girls whose party got fucked up keeps us out the news as murders. That is why I'm leaving the three hundred dollars in the clip so it doesn't look like a robbery. Okay?" Jamya said as she put a comforting hand on Jalyssa's shoulder.

"Okay."

"Finish with the dick wiping and I'm about to wipe the door and shit down with this sanitizer."

The girls cleaned up the room and headed out. Once they got outside Jamya grabbed the keys she took from Chris and went to the car. "Stand right here and look out," she said to Jalyssa.

Jamya used the rag and sanitizer to wipe down the seats where they sat and inside and outside of the door. Once she was done she went to the trunk to satisfy her curiosity from earlier. When she opened the trunk she saw two gym bags. Jamya opened the first bag and saw clothes. She carefully zipped it back up and opened the second one.

Jamya covered her mouth to contain her scream. The bag was filled with cash. *Jackpot,* she thought as she grabbed the bag and closed the trunk. She didn't tell Jalyssa because she was a spicy Latina that would wake up the whole neighborhood with excitement.

"Okay Lyssa. Let's get the hell from around here."

"What's that?"

"Tell you once we get down the street. Let me get the phone," Jamya said as they walked toward a bus stop.

"9-1-1 what's your emergency?"

"Oh my goodness send help!" Jamya said hysterically.

"What's wrong ma'am?"

"I met a guy at the club and went to a hotel with him. Crazy I know but I did. We took some ecstasy and his heart stopped. Please send help!"

"Calm down ma'am. Where are you?"

"The Best Motel room...uh...two...uh...two...thirty-one. Please send help!"

"Okay ma'am. Help is on the way. What's your name?"

"April. April Mutcherson."

"Okay April stay on the line."

"I can't. I need to call my mom. Please just send help," Jamya whined.

"But ma'am-"

Jalyssa hung up and took the battery out of the phone.

"Quite the actress I must say," Jalyssa said with a quiet hand clap.

"Thank you. Thank you very much," she replied with a quick bow.

"Now what's in the bag?"

"Yo, it's full of money."

"What?" Jalyssa said loudly.

"Shhh…we got to play it cool. We'll get into it when we get back to my house but for now we need to get the hell from around here," Jamya paused for a minute and then continued. "I just thought about something."

"What?"

"Guys and Dolls is three blocks away. Let's nix the bus idea and walk that way and call a cab. We'll just look like some of the stripers getting off from work with a gym bag full of our striper clothes versus being down here on a bus."

"True. Good thing we wore our Js tonight," Jalyssa said.

"Hell yeah because our feet would have been burning by now."

When the girls got a block away from the club Jamya called the Yellow Cab number she had saved in her phone. Less than five minutes after they reached the corner by the club their taxi pulled up. They rode in silence to Jamya's house.

Jamya paid the cabbie and they tip toed into the apartment being careful not to wake Cynthia or the girls. They made it to Jamya's room and locked the door. Jamya unzipped the bag and poured the money on the bed. Jalyssa's eyes spread wide and she did a quick salsa as Jamya did her party rock dance.

"Oh my god. I've never seen so much money at one time," Jalyssa said.

"Me either. How much you think it is?"

"I don't know. But I'm down for counting this shit right now."

"Me too. Let me get a notebook so we can keep track," Jamya said opening up her desk drawer.

They counted the money and were smiling from ear to ear the entire time.

"Ninety thousand two hundred and fifty. Now that's a hell of a lick," Jalyssa said.

"Yep. Forty-five thousand one hundred and twenty-five a piece," Jamya said as she laid back on the bed in a fake faint.

"So what time are we going shopping tomorrow?" Jalyssa asked.

"We got to play it cool. This is a lot of money and for some reason I don't see a lame like Chris being the master mind behind some loot like this. We're going to handle business like we have been until we are sure we're in the clear," Jamya said as she came out of her faint.

"Bet," Jalyssa said giving Jamya dap.

"I'm my sister's keeper and I got her back," they said together.

That was their pact since they became best friends. They'd never let anyone or anything come between them. Jamya put her money in a tote box that sat far under her bed while Jalyssa put hers back in the gym bag. The girls went to sleep putting the events of the night behind them.

CHAPTER 2
Emerick Jeffries

Emerick Jeffries grew up with a silver spoon in his mouth in Beverly Hills, California. His parents Mary Ann and Allen Jeffries were the head of an international jewelry chain called Diamont Brut. The business was passed down to them by Mary Ann's father; Adeyemi Okiro. It was rumored that Adeyemi started Diamont Brut with blood diamonds. Though the rumor was never confirmed nor denied, but even after Adeyemi migrated to the United States from Botswana, he made many trips to Botswana and Sierra Leone on business.

As a young boy Emerick worked alongside his grandfather. Adeyemi was a sick man and wanted to ensure his hard work did not go to waste. Though he liked and respected Allen he felt like he did not have the strong arm needed to take Diamont Brut to the next level so he poured into Emerick.

Emerick was sixteen years old when Adeyemi lost his fight with lung cancer. Emerick sat beside Adeyemi's bed while he took his last breath. Before he died Adeyemi told Emerick to ensure his legacy continued and for him to be sure to live life because the angel of death showed no mercy. Emerick carried those words with him; unfortunately they were also his justification for being a womanizer. It didn't matter if they were white, black, Asian, or Latina. Emerick ran through women; usually with no remorse. He took full advantage of being tall, dark, and handsome.

When Emerick turned eighteen his mother told him about a trust fund that his grandfather entrusted her with for him. He'd just got in from celebrating with his friends Bryce and Mike when Mary Ann called to him from the library, "Come in here son."

"Yes ma'am?"

"Have a seat I have something to talk to you about. You turned eighteen today and legally you are a man now. Do not let that go to your head. Your father and I still have the final word on things in this house. Do you understand?"

"Yes ma'am."

"Very good. Now to business. You know that your grandfather single handedly built Diamont Brut. In doing so he was determined to bring our family generational wealth."

Emerick nodded and agreed.

"Your grandfather left you a trust fund that he has been building since he started the company over twenty years ago."

"Whoo."

"Don't get too excited yet. Here are the stipulations that I have placed on the fund. Once you turn twenty one you will receive a monthly allowance of thirty thousand dollars. This will continue until your twenty fifth birthday."

"Then what?"

"One of two things will happen. If you are married in a stable marriage for at least a year you will be granted access to the entire fund less ten million to recycle back into the fund for generations to come."

"Ten million dollars? How much is in the trust?"

"By the time you are twenty five there will be roughly thirty million dollars, give and take."

"Holy shit!"

"Watch your mouth."

"Sorry Mother but that's a lot of money."

"Yes, and that is why you need to be prepared to handle it. That leads me to the second option. If you are not married and settled, then you will receive an increased allowance of fifty thousand a month until that happens."

"That sounds good to me."

"No son that's not. What's good is you getting over this whorish phase."

"Whorish?" he repeated with a laugh.

"You know what I'm talking about boy. Don't play with me," she said with a chuckle.

"I got it Mother," Emerick said as he got up. "I'll make you proud," he added.

"I know son."

Emerick gave his mom a hug and went upstairs to his room. He got on the phone and set up his birthday piece of ass; totally disregarding the conversation he and his mother just had.

****

Emerick graduated high school and went away to the University of Southern California in Los Angeles. Emerick paraded on the campus like he was the man; an attitude brought about by his hefty monthly allowance and the fact that his family had donated to the university for many years. Emerick was more focused on parties and females and less on actually getting an education.

During his junior year Emerick pledged Kappa Alpha Psi. Half way through the year he moved from his single man dorm room into the fraternity house. When he moved into the house he partied like no other; usually with a different young lady of interest.

Emerick's latest victim was Jade Swanson. Jade was the focus of many of the guys on campus. The half Korean and black young lady turned heads with her beauty and confidence. Emerick was used to being with beautiful women so that wasn't what drew him to her. He'd heard that other guys struck out with her because she was a virgin. To Emerick Jade was a challenge, and he enjoyed a challenge.

He approached Jade differently than he had the other young ladies. They'd went out on a couple of dates and he'd actually paid attention to the things she'd say. Emerick realized he'd been doing too much and he made up in his mind play time was over and she had to give up the goods.

The Kappa Alpha Psis were having another one of their shindigs and Emerick invited Jade. By the time Jade got there Emerick was feeling good. He had drunk his share of the kegged beer and had hit a line of cocaine.

"Hey pretty lady," Emerick said greeting her with a kiss on the cheek.

They danced and socialized for a bit and then Emerick invited Jade to his bedroom.

Jade sat on his bed. "I see you cleaned up," she teased.

"Ha ha," he said as he sat down beside her. "You always got jokes," he added with a laugh.

"I'm just saying," Jade said before she joined him in laughter.

"Come here funny lady."

Jade moved closer to Emerick and he grabbed her waist. He pulled her to him, kissed her, and caressed her body.

Jade melted in Emerick's arms. Her breathing quickened when he touched her breast. "Oh Emerick we have to st-"

"Shhh. Let me make you feel good."

"But…"

"No buts. Let me taste you. You know you like it. Lay back."

Emerick had convinced Jade to let him taste her after their second date. He told her that pleasing her was enough for him. He knew once she'd trusted him enough to get that far it was only a matter of time before he'd get the goods.

When Jade laid back on Emerick's bed he raised her skirt and pulled her panties off. Emerick parted her legs and put his face tongue first into her vagina. Jade moaned softly as Emerick worked her toward an orgasm. He licked on Jade's lips and clitoris until her body quivered. He got hard watching her release herself.

Emerick moved up and kissed Jade like he'd done the other times she'd let him taste her. She embraced his kissing and groping not knowing that he'd unbuttoned his pants while he ate her out. He broke his kiss from her, spread her legs, and attempted to enter her.

"Emerick wait. We can't," Jade said when she felt the head

of his penis.

Emerick ignored her plea and leaned over and kissed her again; putting his body weight on her. She attempted to speak but his mouth muffled her words. He moved forward and penetrated her virgin vagina. Her eyes got big from the pain and she attempted to push Emerick off of her with no luck. Jade shrilled with pain as Emerick went in and out of her, pleasing himself with her body.

"Damn girl this is good," he said moments before he released the sperm that filled his penis. He leaned down and attempted to kiss Jade. He gave her a surprised look when she turned her head.

"What's wrong? Don't want to kiss me?"

"What's wrong?" Jade yelled.

"Yeah, calm down."

"I will not. Get your ass off of me Emerick."

Once he did she jumped up and moved to the door.

"Jade wait. What's wrong?" He asked as he went after her.

"Stay the fuck away from me Emerick."

Jade ran out of the Frat house and avoided Emerick like the plague. Emerick didn't think nothing of it and moved about like normal.

Two months after the incident Jade called Emerick.

"Hello," Emerick answered.

"Emerick?"

"Yes."

"This is Jade."

"Hey girl. What's going on?"

"Don't 'hey girl' me. I cannot stand your ass and wish I never had to speak to you again in my life."

"Damn. What you want then?"

"I'm pregnant."

"What you telling me for?" Emerick said arrogantly.

Jade sighed before she started, "I'm going to act like you are really are that stupid. If you do not want your precious mother and/or Dean Ericson to hear about how you raped me I want one hundred thousand dollars. I am leaving school at the end of the semester and I expect to have the money when I leave. So you have three weeks. Got it?"

"Yeah, I got it. But then what Jade?"

"Then what is, I do not believe in abortion so I expect five thousand dollars a month to take care of your kid." Jade paused and then slyly added, "That's chump change for you so I don't foresee a problem."

"Anything else?"

"Yes. Don't take my kindness for weakness Emerick. I don't want to be anywhere in your life, so don't invite me into it?"

"Yeah okay."

"Alright. Talk to you in three weeks," she said matter-a-factly before she hung up.

"Fuck," Emerick said as the reality of what Jade said set in. He wasn't ready to be a father and definitely didn't want his parents to know. Emerick snorted a row of cocaine and then called his mom with a lie to get Jade's money.

CHAPTER 3
Savannah "Liza" Biggs

"Due to the evidence produced, damage caused, and history of one Savannah Elaine Biggs I hereby sentence her to two years at the Cumberland Regional Juvenile Detention Center in Fayetteville North Carolina for assault and battery. During such time Ms. Biggs will undergo counseling and anger management. I also order a psychiatric evaluation to be done and reported back to the court within thirty days from today. It is so ordered," Judge Everson said as she hit her gavel.

Savannah sat with tears in her eyes as she heard her father, Royce let out a sigh and her friend Emily say "No" as the judge read her verdict. Savannah glanced at Royce as she was escorted out of the court room. She was shocked to see his eyes red from crying. Savannah had never seen her father cry and it tore her up inside. Once Savannah got into her transport vehicle she cried; not for her fate but for the pain she'd caused those closest to her.

****

Savannah grew up in Raleigh, North Carolina. She was

raised by her father. Her mother walked out on them when she was three years old. The abandonment had a large part to do with Savannah acting out, though she would never admit it to anyone.

Royce had been an amateur boxer pretty much his whole life and taught Savannah how to fight when she was five. He taught her so that she would be able to protect herself. Unfortunately, for her being an interracial child she fell victim to ridicule; which resulted in her beating lots of asses and her father in court more than he'd liked. Savannah's trouble remained minimal until her luck ran out when she had an altercation with Felicity Waters during her sophomore year of high school.

****

Felicity Waters was what you'd call a "mean girl"; a straight b-i-t-c-h. She was popular and bullied whomever she felt was "beneath" her, which equated to just about everyone. Felicity made it her business to mess with Savannah's friend Emily every chance she got.

That school year Emily had adapted a style that was a mix between gothic and geisha. She dyed her rich auburn hair black, used make up to make her naturally tanned skin pale, wore bright red lipstick, and always wore black and/or gray. Emily didn't care if Felicity or anyone else didn't understand or like her style because she was confident in herself. Her confidence was one reason Felicity did not like Emily and tried so hard to break her down. The other reason Felicity found fault in Emily was that Emily rocked any and all of the styles that Felicity felt were weird. Emily's natural beauty brought out Felicity's green eyed monster.

On the day of Savannah and Felicity's encounter Savannah was waiting for Emily at their normal lunch table. Emily grabbed her tray and was on the way to the table. She was two tables away from their table when Savannah watched Felicity put her backpack in Emily's way. It was like slow motion as Savannah watched Emily trip. She fell one way and her tray flipped and slid the other way.

"Oops," Felicity said followed by hers and everyone else's laughter.

Savannah jumped up and ran over into Felicity's face. "You stupid bitch!"

"It's okay," Emily said with tears in her eyes attempting to hold them in. "She's not even worth it Savannah."

"Ha! I'm not worth it? I'm worth more than either one of y'all," Felicity snared.

Savannah reached down and helped Emily up. "You're right Emily her trifling ass ain't worth no more than the ass she gave the whole football team."

Felicity stood up and squared up with Savannah. "You're just saying that because no one wants to touch your dike ass. Bet you and Emily creepy ass are bumping pussies every night."

"If you know what's good for you you'd get out of my face," Savannah said.

"Chill Felicity, Mrs. Johnson is coming over here," Felicity's friend said from the table.

"Is there a problem girls?" Mrs. Johnson asked when she got to the table.

"No ma'am. I just tripped," Emily said.

"Are you alright?" Mrs. Johnson asked.

"Yes ma'am."

"Okay break this gaggle up girls."

Emily and Savannah turned in one direction and Mrs. Johnson started in the other direction.

"That's right. Move on Emily, you trailer trash slut and your carpet munching half breed girlfriend," Felicity said with a devious smirk.

Savannah saw a tear drop from Emily's eye and she blinked out. Savannah grabbed Emily's tray and smacked Felicity with it. Felicity fell on the ground and Savannah started stomping her. The football coach and another male teacher came and attempted to stop Savannah. The public safety officer finally came and restrained her through her kicking and fighting.

"Calm down young lady," the officer said as he carried her in a reverse bear hug hold.

He carried her through the halls to the main entrance of the school where he exited and put her in the back of his police car. Savannah sat there, kicked, and cursed. Her anger scaled back when an ambulance pulled up in front of the school.

The reality of the situation became apparent and she knew that she'd finally gotten herself in the type of trouble Royce warned her about. She swallowed hard as she thought of how disappointed her father was going to be.

Shortly after the paramedics entered the school, they exited with Felicity strapped to a gurney. Savannah wept as she watched them close the door of the ambulance. That was when she realized that she had a problem with her rage and needed help; quickly.

****

The first few months at Cumberland were rough for Savannah. She couldn't fully get in her rehabilitation because she still had to fight. No one thought the pretty faced "half white girl" could fight so some of the girls tried to push her around. By the sixth month of her being there things started to run smoothly.

Between the weekly letters from Royce and Emily, and her counseling Savannah gained a new prospective on life. She got into the GED program and then took online college classes. By the time Savannah was released she'd completed a financial accounting certificate programs from Columbia University and had begun working on her associate's degree. Savannah went into the facility as an out of control broken child and left as a confident put together young woman.

Emily picked Savannah up on her release day. "Eeekkk," Emily screamed as she ran to hug Savannah. "Oh my god I missed you!"

"Missed you too Em."

They walked to Emily's red convertible Volks Wagon Beetle.

"Oh so you think you hot?" Savannah teased.

"Well...you know," Emily said with a laugh. "But damn, you looking fine then a mug. Big tits, small waist, and you even got an ass now. What you been doing in there? I just seen your ass six months ago and you did not have all of this going on."

Savannah laughed because her body had transformed. She made sure she exercised daily to combat the fattening food in the facility. The biggest shock was Savannah's breast.

She had been a busty girl her whole life. By the fourth grade Savannah wore a 36C bra. Having big breast was nothing to her, but since Emily's last visit Savannah jumped into a J cup. Savannah was glad the uniform covered them because they'd become a distraction to some.

"I just did my normal workout. I did do more squats to plump my bootie though," Savannah added. "So where are we going first?"

"I have a day of pampering planned for us. First stop is to the Target up the street to get you out these busted clothes," Emily exclaimed.

"Hell yeah."

Emily and Savannah went to Target and found Savannah a sundress and sandals before getting manicures, pedicures, and a massage.

Savannah felt like a million bucks and expressed her gratitude to Emily as they ate lunch at a hibachi grill. They talked and Emily filled Savannah in on the missing pieces of her life she didn't write in the letters. Emily was going to school for nursing and stripped at night to live.

"I'd never think you'd strip Em."

"Me either. This chick that was in my class put me on. I was busting my ass at McDonald's to pay my bills plus going to school so I was like 'what the hell'. You know I always liked to perform and do my own thing so that's how I approach it. I get into character and kill it night after night. I plan on doing it until I get out of school and get a nursing job."

"Hey. If it's working out for you do it mama."

"It is," Emily said with a smile.

"You know I got your back," Savannah said.

"Thanks honey. You ready to go?"

"Yeah," Savannah said taking a last sip of her drink.

"Okay. Let's go because I know you're dying to see your pops," Emily said.

"You know I am."

They left the restaurant and headed to Savannah's home. Savannah walked in and was startled by a loud "Surprise". She was face to face with about thirty people in the living space under a "Welcome Home" sign.

"Wow," she managed to squeeze out as her dad scooped her up into a hug.

"Hey baby girl."

"Hey Pops," she replied giving him another hug.

Savannah attempted not to get over whelmed by all of the people. She greeted everyone and was surprised to see that Felicity was there as well.

During Savannah's counseling at Cumberland, one of her

exercises was accepting your wrong and asking for forgiveness. That message impacted Savannah in a way that she didn't expect. Her course of action was to write Felicity a letter. Savannah expressed a sincere apology for the pain she caused; physically, mentally, and emotionally. Savannah never knew how Felicity felt about her letter because she never responded. Seeing Felicity reassured Savannah that she was forgiven.

Savannah began to cry as she saw the damage that she left Felicity to live with. She'd caused permanent damage to her eye orbit and the entire right side of her face drooped.

"I'm so glad you came," Savannah said as she offered Felicity a hug.

"Me too," Felicity said as she hugged Savannah. "I cannot stay but I felt the need to come. Let's put this behind us and move on."

"Okay."

"Good luck Savannah."

"Thanks Felicity. That means a lot to me."

What Savannah did not know was Felicity had gone to counseling as well after a failed suicide attempt. After the incident between her and Savannah, Felicity was knocked off her "mean girl" high horse. She experienced firsthand how the people she tortured felt. All of Felicity's so called friends abandoned her and left her feeling hopeless. She took half a bottle of her pain pills in attempt to end her life. Luckily her mother got to her and called 9-1-1 before the overdose was fatal.

During Felicity's counseling, she too was coached to take responsibility of her actions. She'd realized her injuries were caused because of years and years of her treating people like dirt. She received Savannah's letter while she was in her rebuilding stage and felt like it was a sign from God. Felicity did not respond to the letter because she was not strong enough at that time and was still finding herself.

Felicity worked at the Kroger that Savannah's father frequently shopped at. Every time she was working when he went in he'd be sure to make small talk and ask her how she was doing. That was his way of attempting to right Savannah's wrong.

A month before Savannah's release Felicity felt urged to ask about Savannah. Royce was shocked that she'd asked but he told her that Savannah was doing well and was soon to be released. He smiled as he accepted her genuine "that's good". When Royce was shopping for the food for the welcome home celebration he'd invited Felicity to attend; hence how she and Savannah were able to have their interaction.

Felicity left the party and Savannah mingled with the

other guest. She was thrilled that so many people had taken the time out of their lives to celebrate her release. By the end of the evening Savannah was beat. She and Royce ended the night on the couch watching movies.

CHAPTER 4
Time For A Change

Jamya and Jalyssa laid low with their head close to the ground after the hotel mishap. They'd taken all precautions Jamya could think of to ensure that they were not linked to Chris' death. The day after, they'd thrown the burner phone, Chris' keys, and the gym bag in the river. They also played it cool and did not spend ridiculous amounts of money.

Jamya was lying across her bed listening to music when Jalyssa came in. "Hey girl. I didn't even hear the door," she said.

"Yeah, your moms let me in," Jalyssa said out of breath.

"What's up?"

"The streets are talking."

Jamya sat up, "What happened?"

"That money that Chris had. It was Big Pig's."

"Big Pig's…Shit."

Big Pig was a big time dealer who had the majority of Chicago on lock.

"Chris had hit one of his spots the night we met him. We dodged the police with your plan but Pig ain't happy. He's been watching the news and is looking for the broad Chris was partying with. It's a matter of time until they trace his tracks to the club and find out it was actually two chicks instead of one. What are we going to do Mya?"

"First, you're going to calm down. I hope you weren't this uptight when you got the info because your ass look about guilty. Play it cool. We have the upper hand right now. Everybody around here thinks we're plain college girls, trying to get out of the hood. Are you still down for the move we talked about?"

"Hell yeah."

Jamya and Jalyssa had talked about moving to California after they graduated. They had been saving money and planned to make the move in the summer.

"Okay. We're going to have to move our plan up. This is how we are going to play this. Tell everyone we both got picked up to interview at that web agency you've been talking about getting on at. The interview is on next Monday so we're going to take the train. What's today?"

"Tuesday."

"We're going to take the train on Thursday. Be extra excited that they picked both of us up so people will carry the news of the college girls catching a break. This will do two things; keep us off the radar as street girls and it'll be our way out. Make sure you talk about how you think we are going to get it because they're even paying for our train ticket and hotel."

"You are so damn smart and conniving," Jalyssa said with a smile. "I'm glad you're on my side."

Jamya laughed at Jalyssa but she knew she was for real.

"Mom! Mom! Mom!" Jamya yelled.

"What the hell Jamya? What are you calling me like that for? You alright?"

"Yes! I'm better than alright! So me and Jalyssa have been putting in applications and we both got interviews at a web agency!"

"That's great!" Cynthia exclaimed as she hugged both of them. "I'm so proud of you girls. Where is it? Downtown?"

"Not exactly," Jamya said.

"Not exactly? Then where is it?" Cynthia asked looking puzzled.

"It's in LA."

"Los Angeles LA?"

"Yes ma'am," Jamya said as she watched the excitement leave her mother's face.

"Y'all want to go way out there?" she asked with a sigh.

"It's a great opportunity Mom."

"Yeah Mama Cynthia," Jalyssa cosigned.

Cynthia forced a smile, "Okay but I'll miss you two."

"Don't worry Mama Cynthia. We'll make enough money to come back and visit," Jalyssa added.

"Oh my how the two of you have grown. Though I'll miss you, I wish y'all luck. When is the interview?"

"It's Monday," Jalyssa said.

"Yeah, we're taking the train on Thursday. They're even taking care of travel and lodging. I think we already got the job for real. They'd be crazy not to hire us. Especially since we were in the top five percent of our class," Jamya added.

"Wow. Sounds like you have it to me. I'm happy for the both of you but I'm going to cry when you leave though. Glad you'll be together."

"Of course," they said in unison.

"Well, Mama Cynthia I have to get home and tell my mama the good news," Jalyssa said before she gave Cynthia a hug. "Call you later Mya," she said as she left out of the room.

Cynthia left out of the room and went back to cooking dinner. Jamya laid back on her bed and tears welled up behind her eyelids. She hated to tell her mother such an elaborate lie but she could not risk bringing trouble to her mom and sisters. Jamya loved the streets but she knew she had to get a hold of her recklessness; quick fast and in a hurry.

****

Emerick went on a downhill spiral after Jade left school. He tried to act tough but the baby situation had him bothered. Emerick's cocaine habit got worst. He used the powder to bury his feelings and his schooling paid for it heavily. Emerick spent more time out of class than he did in. Half way through the semester he was called to the academics department to speak to his advisor Mrs. Avery.

"Mr. Jeffries I've gotten several complaints on your class attendance. You are at risk of failing four of your six classes at this time. I've reviewed the documentation submitted by your professors and the only problem seems to be your attendance because your grades are impeccable. Listen Mr. Jeffries you are a bright young man. I'm not sure what exactly is going on but I need for you to pull it together if you want to continue your education here. Understood?"

"Yes ma'am," Emerick said.

"Good, now go make it to class," Mrs. Avery added.

Emerick left out of her office but class was not on his mind. Instead he went back to the frat house and got wasted. He was passed out in his room when the fraternity president Devin entered his room. Devin called Emerick's name but he did not move. He shook Emerick, "Bruh. Bruh. You alright?"

he asked as he put his face to his chest. Devin began to panic with the faintness of Emerick's heartbeat. He grabbed his phone and called 9-1-1. While Devin waited for the paramedics to come he grabbed Emerick's emergency contact sheet. He pulled the form from his filing cabinet and called Emerick's mother. Mary Ann dropped everything and had her driver take her to the hospital.

Devin followed the ambulance and waited until she got there. It took Mary Ann almost an hour and a half to get to the hospital through the midday traffic. Devin greeted Mary Ann in the waiting room.

"Good afternoon Mrs. Jeffries."

"What has happened Devin? Has the doctors said anything yet?"

"I'm not sure of the medical mumbo jumbo but pretty much he is in a cocaine induced coma."

"Cocaine?"

"Yes ma'am."

"There is no way. Not my Emerick," Mary Ann said sternly.

Devin stood in silence because he knew for sure that Emerick used cocaine; he'd witnessed him snort before.

"What room is he in Devin?"

"He's in room eight Mrs. Jeffries."

"Thank you for contacting me and coming to the hospital with my boy."

"No problem Mrs. Jeffries, he's my brother."

Mary Ann forced a smile to hide her hurt and disappoint in Emerick.

"I have to go back to campus to do an incident report of the situation. I will be back to check on E later."

"If it's at all possible can you please omit the hear say of the cocaine involvement?"

"I don't know about that Mrs. Jeffries."

"I understand but know that if you could find a way to perhaps mention you came here and left the matters in my hands, which you have, you can omit what you'd heard. That is all I am saying. IF you could do that and email me a copy of your report there would be a hefty present delivered to you on tomorrow," Mary Ann said as she grabbed a business card out of her purse.

She handed Devin the card and continued, "My email is listed below. Thank you again…son. You have a good day and I hope to hear from you later."

Mary Ann walked off leaving Devin to process her request. She went to the nurses' station and spoke to the attending nurse who instructed her how to get to Emerick's room.

Mary Ann wept when she saw Emerick lying there lifeless with the machines beeping around him. She stood near his bed and replayed the conversation she had with Devin. *Why would he start using drugs? I've taught him better than that.* "Damn it son," she whispered as she took his hand.

Mary Ann was still in deep thought when the doctor walked in.

"Hello. I am Doctor St. John and you are?"

She wiped the last of her tears and said, "I am Mary Ann Jeffries; Emerick's mother."

"Nice to meet you Mrs. Jeffries."

"Same here. What is going on with my son doctor?"

"Well Mrs. Jeffries, your son is in a cocaine induced comatose state right now. There is really no way to tell how long Mr. Jeffries will remain in this state. It could be anywhere from hours to months." Mary Ann let out a sigh as Doctor St. John continued, "However, his vitals are stable which is very promising."

"Is there anything I can do?"

"No ma'am. It is really just a waiting game at this point."

"Very well," Mary Ann said in a defeated tone.

"His nurse on duty is Barbara. She will be in shortly to record his vitals. Feel free to let her know anything you would need to make your stay more comfortable for I am sure you will be staying," he said with a soft smile.

"Yes, I will be. Thank you very much doctor."

"You are welcome Mrs. Jeffries," he said before he exited the room.

Mary Ann called Allen at the office and gave him the update on Emerick. When he suggested that he skip a meeting with a buyer to come to the hospital she responded with, "You handle the business and I will handle it here. We must keep production up. I will keep you posted to any changes." Allen agreed and they hung up. Mary Ann then called her misses, Amyra and gave her instructions on things to pack in an overnight bag for her. She then sent her driver Cecil to fetch her things.

Mary Ann stayed by Emerick's side all that day and that night. The hospital staff gave her a cot to sleep on in the room; nothing like the pillow top mattress she was accustomed to. Mary Ann finally fell asleep after she tossed and turned for hours.

It was around three a.m. when Mary Ann was awakened by soft grunts. She opened her eyes and saw Emerick pulling at the cords that were attached to him.

"Emerick," she said still half asleep.

"Mother," Emerick said dazed. "What is going on? Why am I hooked up to all of these machines? Hell, why am I in the hospital?"

"You had an incident. Stop pulling at those," she said as she moved toward him.

"An incident?"

"Yes, an incident that was a result from your drug use. What is wrong with you Emerick? You were raised better than that young man."

"Mother…"

"Don't mother me. I am grateful that you are awake but know that you will be checked into a rehabilitation center as soon as you are released from here."

"I do not need rehab."

"I would have thought the same thing before you were in a cocaine induced coma Emerick. This is not up for discussion. As it stands now you are not fit to run the business. That son is unacceptable."

"And there it goes…the business. That is all you've ever been worried about."

"That is not true Emerick so stop talking such noise. I will go get the nurse so that they are aware that you are awake." She walked out of the room and left the conversation where it stood.

Mary Ann made sure that Emerick got a hold of his drug problem. Emerick stayed in the hospital for nearly a week after he woke from his comatose state. By the time he was released Mary Ann had had all of his things packed up and shipped to their home as well as had him withdrawn from school. Emerick was not happy and attempted to fight his mother tooth and nail, but he did not stand a chance against her overbearing personality. He gave up the fight because not only did his mother control the money he received but he also had Jade and the growing fetus that he had to worry about. He had eight months left until his twenty first birthday, he had to keep his mother happy until he started to get his trust fund allowances.

After his release from the hospital Emerick was admitted to a private rehabilitation center. He went through the six month program like a champ. He knocked the desire for the coke from his mind during his stay and hoped it would remain gone, especially since he was not ready to give up partying.

****

Things were going well for Savannah on the outside. She'd gotten a waitressing job at the club where Emily worked. The owner tried hard to persuade her to strip but she politely declined. Though Savannah loved to dance around her room she had no desire to show her skills (or lack thereof) to a room full of men. The tips were good on top of the eight dollar hourly rate so she was happy.

One night while Savannah was working she was propositioned by a gentleman named Sebastian. "You are a beautiful woman Savannah," he said when she returned with his drink.

"Thank you," she said hesitantly waiting on his next statement. She got hit on constantly and had prepared herself to fire back on him if he came out of his mouth disrespectfully.

"My name is Sebastian Erickson," he said handing her a card. "I'm a photographer and would love to photograph you."

"Oh yeah?" Savannah said as she looked over the card.

"Yes. I love your look," he said looking her up and down with focus on her boobs that were displayed in her half shirt.

"Since you're scouting in a strip club I'm going to assume that you are not looking for girls to model three piece suits," Savannah said looking at Sebastian suspiciously.

Sebastian chuckled, "No my employer does not want the girls to model three pieces suits. He is more focused on topless or sexier attire in the photo shoots. I think he would love you because you fit into what he's looking for."

"Thank you but no thank you," Savannah said as she started to walk off.

"Wait. Wait. Please hear me out. I may say something that interest you. The pay and benefits are good. Please just give me two minutes."

Savannah stopped and turned toward him, "Two minutes. I'm listening."

"We will fly you to Los Angeles, put you up in a hotel, cover your food, and as well as give you one thousand dollars."

"You got to be shitting me. That shit sounds too good to be true. What's the catch?"

"The catch is you're a beautiful voluptuous woman that men will flock to. In turn my employer will get reimbursed in revenue. If you don't mind I would like to take a picture of you on my phone to send to him."

"For what?"

"Though I see a lot of women who fit into my image for the photo shoots, ultimately it's his decision because he writes the checks."

"Oh."

"No pressure. You can still think it over but I do want you to be in the lineup for his decision because I would love to photograph you. Your features are extraordinary."

"Let me serve my other tables and I will let you know," Savannah said.

"Okay beautiful. I will be right here until you return."

Sebastian's words danced around in Savannah's head as she took the food and drinks to the other tables. While Savannah was at the bar Emily came in to work. She stopped by the bar to speak to Savannah.

"Em! I'm so glad you're here," Savannah exclaimed when she saw her. Emily stood looking confused. Savannah pulled Emily by the arm to the restroom.

"What is going on Savannah?"

"Dude at the table to the right of the stage wants to photograph me; talking about sending me to Cali. Airfare, food, and hotel included, plus paying me a thousand dollars."

"What? What's the catch?"

"Exactly. They want me to pose topless. What you think?"

"Shit I'd do it! Where that fucker at?" Emily said acting like she was going out the door.

"You're a trip Em," Savannah said laughing. "So you don't see a problem with it?"

"Hell nah! I strip for less than that. As long as they hold their end of the bargain and you get paid with no expense out of your pocket I say go for it. You've always wanted to go to Cali. Plus you are not one of those big boob ditzy bimbos. You know how to take care of yourself."

"Thanks Em," Savannah said as she gave Emily a hug.

Savannah went back to work feeling better about the situation. She allowed Sebastian to take her picture and send it to his employer Joshua Roderick. Joshua immediately responded that he wanted Savannah at whatever cost; a fact that Sebastian left out since she was already sold on the original agreement.

Savannah and Sebastian met for lunch the next day. He filled her in on the job which was her being photographed for Joshua's magazine Passion House. Savannah informed Sebastian that she'd never done any modeling and wasn't one hundred percent comfortable with posing naked. He calmed her nerves by letting her know it would be a closed set and he'd have options such as bra and bikini tops on set for her. Savannah signed an agreement that outlined the shoot for Passion House as well as an agreement for complete accommodations.

Royce was not happy about Savannah's decision to do the photo shoot. He expressed his concerns about it being all the way in California and possibly dangerous. Savannah took into account Royce's concerns but still left the following day for Los Angeles.

CHAPTER 5
New Beginnings

Jamya and Jalyssa left on the train that Thursday for their make believe interview. Neither of the girls had ever left out of Illinois and their excitement level was through the roof. They looked out the windows of the train in awe the entire trip when they were not napping.

Though the girls took the forty-two hour trip like champs, they were ready to get off of the train by the time they arrived at Union Station. Jamya and Jalyssa briefly took in the sights of the train station as they walked out to grab a cab. "Yo, Mya this is so different from Chicago," Jalyssa said looking at the sunny fresh scenery.

A handsome young Indian man approached them, "Hello beautiful ladies I am Rah. Do you need a cab today?"

"Yes we do," Jamya responded.

Rah grabbed their roller suitcases. Then he attempted to grab Jamya's backpack that held bundles of cash. "I'll keep this one," she said. He gave her a smile and head nod as he lead them to his cab. They got in the cab as he put their bags in the trunk. "Where to?" Rah asked when he sat down in the cab.

"The Omni Hotel off of Olive Street," Jamya said.

Rah drove Jamya and Jalyssa to the Omni. They checked in and went up to their room.

"Damn this is nice Mya," Jalyssa said as they entered the room. They spared no expense with the two bedroom hotel suite.

"Yes. We'll be living large for the next few days," Jamya responded.

"Hell yeah! Let the vacation begin!"

They called and checked in at home, showered, and relaxed a bit before hitting the downtown strip for food and shopping.

Jamya and Jalyssa partied and took in the sights of LA on their trip but they also handled business. They checked on some jobs while they were there. They put in applications and submitted resumes to some companies but nothing looked promising. Though the job hunt seemed to be a bust they found an affordable two bedroom two bathroom apartment.

They returned to Los Angeles a week after their "interview". Their move was bitter sweet. They hated to leave their family but they were also excited about the change of scenery. Everyone bought their story about their job offers and they felt confident that Big Pig would never connect them to his money.

"Honey I'm home," Jalyssa said in her version of a Ricky Ricardo voice when she and Jamya entered into the empty apartment. They did not mind that they had nothing in the apartment except for the bags that they brought with them because that was the first apartment either of them had without their mothers. Jamya put the bags she had down, laid on the carpet, and did a "snow angel". Jalyssa laughed as she joined her.

"Lyssa this is the start of the next chapter of our lives."

"I know. We're finally where we dreamt of being. I hope LA is ready for us."

"Hell yeah!" Jamya exclaimed.

They took their things to their rooms and then called a cab to take them to Wal-Mart. They bought food, household items, and air mattresses to hold them over until they got real beds. As they walked up the breezeway, two women walked up as well. The two women went to the apartment across from theirs.

"Oh, you're our new neighbors. I'm Diamond and this is my sister Sapphire," one of the ladies said as she extended her hand to Jamya.

Jamya shook her hand the best she could holding the bags, "I'm Jamya and this is Jalyssa."

"Well, welcome," Diamond said.

"Where are you guys from because you do not have a Cali accent?" Sapphire asked.

"We're from Chicago," Jamya said.

"That's cool," Diamond said with a soft smile. "Nice to meet you and we're across the hall if you need anything," she added.

"Thank you," Jamya and Jalyssa both said.

Diamond and Sapphire went into their apartment. Jamya and Jalyssa got settled in their apartment and prepared for their new beginning.

Later that evening as Jamya and Jalyssa sat in their apartment strategizing their next moves there was a knock on the door. Jamya went to the door after their brief "who the hell is that" stare. Jalyssa was not far behind her with a bat in her hand.

"Who is it?" Jamya asked.

"It's Diamond," came from the other side of the door.

Jalyssa relaxed from her batter stance and Jamya opened the door.

"Hey. I hope I didn't disturb you guys."

"No, you're good. What's up?" Jamya responded.

"My sister and I are going out tonight and I wondered if you guys wanted to go. I figured you guys would like to get out of this apartment for a while."

"Hell yeah," Jalyssa exclaimed in the background.

Jamya laughed at her and then said, "I was about to say let me ask Jalyssa but I guess that means she's down, so yeah we'll go. Thanks for asking."

"No problem. We'll be leaving around ten. It's a nice night club with lots of money floating around so dress nice. Whenever you guys are ready you can just come over."

"Okay. We'll see you later then," Jamya said as Diamond walked off.

She closed the door and was face to face with an overly excited Jalyssa. "That's what I'm talking about. Let's get sexy than a motherfucker and see about this money that's in the club."

"Chill Lyssa. We gotta play things cool. We don't know them chicks for real. We can't let them get an inkling of our hustle. We'll scope it out tonight with them, then we'll go by ourselves on that money tip."

"Okay cool."

Jamya shook her head because Jalyssa was always ready to just jump and Jamya always had to talk her off of the ledge.

Jamya's phone rang and she lit up to see it was her mother. "Hey Mama...We're doing good...Yeah. We're actually going out with our neighbors tonight...We're always careful Mama…Yes ma'am…I'll tell her…Miss you too Mama. Love you." Jamya let Jalyssa know that her mother said hello and then begun her planning process for the night.

They got dressed in their outfits they got on their initial trip to LA. Jamya wore a mini sequined black dress and black red bottom pumps. Jalyssa wore black hot pants, a black, white, and silver top, and red Jimmy Choos. They did their hair and makeup looking like a million bucks when they stepped out of their apartment. They went over and knocked on Diamond and Sapphire's door. Diamond answered, "Looking good ladies. Come in."

"Thanks," they said as they walked into the apartment.

It was like day and night from their apartment. Diamond and Sapphire had chic modern furniture with paintings and sculptures accenting the living room.

"Damn this is nice chica," Jalyssa said.

"Thanks," Diamond said with a smile. "It's just a little something something."

This is a little more than a little something something, Jamya thought.

They followed Diamond into the living room. "Excuse me for a second. I have to finish getting ready. You can have a seat," she said as she walked towards the back of the apartment. Jamya heard her say, "Sapph the girls are here."

Jamya continued to look around the apartment at the expensive décor. "What do these hoes do?" she whispered to Jalyssa.

"I don't know but we need to be down cause this place is nice as hell," Jalyssa whispered back.

"Y'all can turn on the television if you want," Diamond yelled from the bedroom. "The remote's on the end table."

Jalyssa grabbed the remote for the sixty inch flat screen and turned it on. She channel surfed until she got to the movie Set It Off. "Oh Mya, our shit's on." They'd watched that movie at least a hundred times together. They were all into the movie when Diamond and Sapphire came into the living room.

They were smoking hot looking like they'd just stepped off somebody's runway. *These bitches are some label whores for real. I like their style though. This relationship may turn out to be promising,* Jamya thought. They both were already stunning with their five nine and five ten model builds, smooth chocolate skin, and flowing hair, but their outfits were amazing. Sapphire was wearing Balmain from head to toe and Diamond had on a Gucci dress and Tom Ford stilettos. As if their labels didn't speak money already, their blinged out jewelry pulled the looks together.

"Damn y'all look good. Make us look like chopped

liver," Jamya said.

"Thank you and no we don't. You guys look good," Diamond said.

Sapphire being the conceded one of the group said, "Well…" with a "I know I'm the shit" smirk.

"I just have one question," Jalyssa started. "What y'all hoes do? Shit, between this apartment and y'all clothes it has to be some good shit."

Jamya gave Jalyssa a scolding look. "What? I'm just saying. You know you want to know too."

Diamond laughed while Sapphire didn't crack a smile.

"Let's just say we're in the sponsorship business," Diamond said.

"Let's go," Sapphire cut in to hush her up.

I'm going to have to talk to Diamond when Sapphire is not around, Jamya thought as she got up from the couch.

They all left the apartment and went down to Sapphire's all black Audi.

"This is nice," Jamya said to Sapphire.

"Thanks. This is my baby. The only dude that's loyal," she replied with a laugh.

"It be like that sometimes," Jalyssa added in.

"Thanks again for inviting us," Jamya said. "So where are we going?"

Enough

"Club Night Life," Diamond said. "It should be fun."

****

Once Emerick completed rehab he moved back home with Mary Ann and Allen. He did all he could to fly right. He took online classes to finish his degree while he worked alongside his father at Diamont Brut in preparation of taking over the company in the future. Against Mary Ann's wishes Allen had planned to turn the company over to Emerick well before he turned twenty five. Though Emerick knew the workings of Diamont Brut inside and out he hoped his mother's persuasive nature kicked in and Allen remained in charge. He was not ready to devote every second of everyday to the business. He wasn't too worried though because Mary Ann always got her way; she paid the cost to be the boss.

Emerick put on his MEK jeans, Armani Exchange t-shirt, Gucci shoes, and Armani sports coat. "Damn I look good," he said standing in front of the 360 mirror in his dressing room. It was his birthday and his friend Mike was taking him out. Emerick sprayed himself with cologne and gave himself another once over. "Oh damn. I almost forgot my watch." Mary Ann and Allen gave him a Diamont Brut exclusive for his birthday. The watch was platinum and encrusted with yellow and white diamonds. His one of a kind piece was worth forty-nine thousand dollars.

Mike called Emerick as he finished clasping the watch, "What up man?"

"Shit. I'm about five minutes from your crib. Hope you're ready. You know you're worst than a female."

"Whatever man. I'm actually ready."

"Oh shit. Let me find out your ass turned twenty-one and got your shit together."

"So your ass got jokes I see."

"Just a little," Mike said with a little chuckle.

"Whatever man. Hurry up," Emerick said before hanging up.

He'd just got downstairs when Amyra opened the door for Mike.

"Yo bro you looking clean man."

"Thanks bruh," Emerick said giving him a handshake and chest bump.

Mary Ann and Allen came into the foyer. "Hey Mr. and Mrs. Jeffries."

"Michael," Mary Ann said in a poised tone.

"Hey Mike," Allen said. "You boys ready to hit the city?" he asked.

"Yes Mr. Jefferies."

"Make sure to be careful," he added.

Mary Ann gave Emerick a side eye look with Allen's

comment.

"Yes sir," Mike replied.

"We will Pop."

"Your mother and I got a little something for you that might help with you all's evening."

Allen gave Emerick a small box. He shook the box and heard a rattle. *What? Matching cuff links or a necklace?* Emerick opened the box and pulled out a key fob. He pulled it out and saw the Mauserati emblem. "No way!" he exclaimed with a big smile. He gave both his parents hugs.

"Where is it?" he asked sounding like a little kid.

"Out in the garage."

Emerick took off with Mike right behind him. Their mouths dropped when they got to the garage to the white Mauserati with a peanut butter interior.

"Whoa," Emerick said.

"Yo bruh, this shit's fire.

"Hell yeah! Guess we're taking my ride tonight."

"Fuck yeah!"

Emerick started the car and smiled as it purred like a kitten. "So where are we going?" Emerick asked.

"That new club, Club Night Life.

"I heard that spot be jumping and the hoes be out there."

"Exactly. That's why we're going. Let's celebrate this birthday royally."

CHAPTER 6
Model Behavior

Savannah was a natural talent when it came to modeling. All Sebastian kept telling her was "beautiful", "nice", or "lovely" as he snapped his camera.

"You really become someone else when the camera flashes," he said.

"Thank you. I embrace my inner Liza charm."

"Liza?"

"Yeah, Liza Minnelli," Savannah said proudly.

Sebastian gave a slow head nod to her response.

Savannah was glad it went well because she was nervous. Emily came through for her as always. She'd given Savannah pointers which included thinking about her favorite actor or actress and embodying the energy they display in their work. Emily reminded her modeling and dancing were no more than acting. Savannah loved Liza Minnelli; she enjoyed the classics more so than the modern movies. It also helped that Sebastian kept his word and had collections of swim suits for her to choose from so she didn't feel completely exposed.

Savannah and Sebastian were going through the pictures

on his computer screen when Joshua came to the shoot.

"Superb," he said when he got to the computer. "Hello beautiful I'm Joshua, but you can call me Josh."

"Savannah," Savannah responded as Joshua kissed her hand.

"You're a natural," he said.

"Isn't she?" Sebastian added.

"Sebastian I want a scene with her, Bubbles, and Tina when they get here," Joshua said as he studied Savannah's photos. "I want it to be a hot pool scene."

"Okay. I can see it. The three of them will be great."

"Great. I'm going to leave you to your creative business," Joshua said to Sebastian. "Very nice to meet you Savannah. Myself, my team, and some of the girls will be getting together tonight. If you do not have any plans I would love for you to join us."

Any plans? The only plan I had was to lay my ass in that comfortable bed at the hotel. That is all so hell yeah, Savannah thought.

"I do not have any plans so I don't see why not."

"Great. I'll have my assistant Stacey get with you. She is on her way here now."

"Okay."

"Until later," Joshua said on his way out.

Savannah was surprised that Bubbles and Tina weren't some ditzy models. Bubbles came from Nevada and Tina from Georgia, each with lots of life experiences. After their pool scene they "schooled" her on the business as well as Joshua.

"He's a boob man and let's face it honey, you are all boobs," Tina told Savannah. "No matter how charming he is keep it professional. Remember that and you'll be fine. I can tell you're a fighter though."

"Thanks Tina."

"Anytime tuts."

Stacey came into the changing space at that time. "Great job ladies. Savannah I see why Josh is so excited about you; you did awesome."

"Thanks," Savannah said.

"When you ladies are done getting dressed we can go," Stacey called out to Savannah, Tina, and Bubbles.

Savannah and the ladies pushed pause on their conversation and got dressed. The driver took them to the hotel.

"Eat and relax. I'll be outside of the hotel at ten to get you," Stacey said as Savannah, Bubbles, and Tina got out of the car.

Savannah did just that before tearing up her suitcase.

She'd packed a going out outfit. She just hoped her North Carolina fashion held up to the glam of the Los Angeles night life. She put on a corset top, pencil skirt, and pumps. She then put on minimal makeup, framed her face with her blonde highlighted hair, and put on some dangling earrings. Though Savannah didn't know if she was LA nights fine, she knew she looked damn good.

Savannah's phone went off while she gave herself the final once over. When she picked it up she saw that she'd received picture mail from Sebastian. She was overwhelmed with emotion as she saw the pictures and read his message. *"You did a wonderful job and I'm glad I am the one privileged enough to introduce the world to Liza Biggs."*

"Liza Biggs. I like it!"

Savannah put some extra bounce in her step and linked up with Bubbles and Tina in the lobby. They waited until Stacey pulled up in her Lexus SUV.

"You ladies ready for a night of fun?" she asked once they got in.

"Hell yeah," Tina said.

"Good! We work hard to play harder. Next stop Club Night Life."

CHAPTER 7
First Encounters

Night life was a lot different in Los Angeles than in Chicago. Jamya thought they'd pulled up to a movie premier or awards ceremony instead of a night club. Everyone was nicely dressed and there was a line around the building. *Definitely must be a hot spot,* Jamya thought as she and Jalyssa looked at each other in amazement.

Sapphire pulled up to the valet. "You guys ready for a fun evening?" Diamond asked as she fixed her cleavage.

"Yes," Jamya said.

"Hell yeah," Jalyssa said.

The valet opened up the front and rear passenger door and then moved to the driver side to let Sapphire and Jalyssa out. Jamya and Jalyssa strutted along side of Diamond and Sapphire as they bypassed the long line and walked up a separate roped area. The ladies were stopped by a big sexy Samoan man. Jamya was at a loss for words because she had the biggest celebrity crush on The Rock and buddy could have passed for his brother.

"Hey ladies. How's it going?"

"Hey Eli," Diamond and Sapphire said.

"I see you brought some friends," he said with a smile that could be on any toothpaste commercial.

"Yeah. This is Jamya and this is Jalyssa."

"Nice to meet you beautiful ladies. Can I see your IDs."

"Really Eli? They are with us," Sapphire said.

"Sapph, you know we go way back and I trust the hell out of you, but this is my gig. I don't have the boss in my pocket like you do so I have to be on the up and up."

Jamya and Jalyssa handed Eli their IDs.

"Illinois. You here visiting?"

"No, we relocated here," Jamya said flirtatiously.

"Uh hum," came from a group of impatient girls behind them.

"Welcome to Cali ladies. I hope you have a good time tonight," Eli said removing the rope at the entrance.

They stepped through double door. Jamya and Jalyssa followed Diamond and Sapphire to the entry booth.

"Hello ladies," the woman working the booth said.

"Hi," they all said.

"Four please," Diamond said as she opened her clutch bag.

"That will be four hundred please."

"You don't have to-." Jamya started before Diamond cut

her off.

"It's not a problem."

"Are you sure?" Jamya asked as Diamond gave the lady four crisp hundred dollar bills.

"Yes. You're good. Let's call it a welcome to Cali gift," she said with a smile.

"Thank you," Jamya said.

They moved past the booth then through the security point before they entered the lavish ten thousand square foot club.

"This shit's hella nice," Jalyssa commented.

Jamya nodded her head agreeing.

"Yes it is. Diamond and I are regulars. Wait until you see the VIP area," Sapphire said.

"Yeah there's water fountains in there and everything," Diamond added.

"Damn," Jamya said though she wasn't surprised because the setup was nice from the lighting, to the marble top tables, and oversized chairs.

"Hey Sapphire. Mark just asked if you'd arrived," a petite red head walked up to Sapphire and said.

"Hey Candy. Where is he?"

"Waiting on you in VIP section one."

"Okay. Thanks."

"Who's Mark?" Jamya whispered to Diamond.

"He's Sapphire's main interest."

Main? Jamya thought.

"He's part owner of this place," she said.

"Oh wow."

"What he look like? He got a brother?" Jalyssa asked.

Diamond laughed but Jamya knew she was serious.

Sapphire led them as they made their way through the crowd to the VIP section. Sapphire spoke to a Rick Ross (before his weight loss) look-a-like and he let them all in. Sapphire was approached and kissed on the cheek by a sexy medium build guy with a California tan, smooth face, curly blonde hair, and sky blue eyes.

He greeted Diamond and said, "Sapphire please introduce me to your beautiful friends."

"This is Jamya and this is Jalyssa. They just moved here from Chicago."

"Chicago? What a lovely city. Such culture. Nice to meet you."

"Thank you," Jalyssa said.

"Same here," Jamya said.

Mark ushered them to the sitting area that over looked the club. *Diamond was right when she said there was money up in here. Look at those outfits and those bottles being ordered from the bar,*

Jamya thought as she sat taking in the scene.

****

When Emerick and Mike got to Club Night Life they were like kids in a candy store. There were so many beautiful women that they could not focus on any one of them. They made their way to VIP section two next to where Jamya and her gang were.

When Emerick entered the area he was surprised to see that some of his frat brothers and some half naked women were there. He turned to Mike with the biggest grin on his face. The first to wish him a happy birthday was Devin. Emerick was happy to see him because he had not seen him since the hospital.

"What up bro? Looking good. Happy big two one."

"Thanks man," Emerick replied with a gigantic smile.

Emerick put the waitress to work getting drinks immediately after speaking to everyone.

"Here's the keys bruh because I plan on getting shit faced tonight," Emerick said to Mike.

"Shit, that's what you do best. It's your motherfucking birthday though. Enjoy yourself; drink, dance, and get at these bitches."

Unlimited Margaritas, Martinis, and Ciroc were perks of VIP, but Emerick wanted to go big for his birthday. He ordered ten bottles of Armand De Brignac, not worrying about the hefty price tag of the three hundred dollar champagne. When the champagne came Mike made a toast. "This dude right here is my motherfucking boy! For real. We've been through a lot during our fifteen years of friendship. He's the closest thing possible to a blood brother to me. I'm glad everyone came to celebrate his birthday tonight. Love ya bruh. Happy birthday."

Just then the DJ came across the microphone. "This is motherfucking Kane on the ones and twos. Everybody looking good out there on tonight. Happy birthday shout out to Emerick Jeffries. What up E?" Kane said pointing to the VIP section. "Ladies he's single so make sure y'all show him some love tonight. Let's continue this party. Ladies this is for you," he said as he played Beyonce's *Drunk In Love.*

One of the ladies that was with Devin and the crew sat Emerick down and got her Beyonce on all over him. She did all but suck his dick during the song. Emerick sat and enjoyed it all.

****

Savannah, Bubbles, Tina, Stacey, Joshua, and Sebastian walked into Club Night Life as DJ Kane was giving Emerick his birthday shout out. Savannah had never been to any club other than the strip club she worked at (a downfall of being locked up so young). She was full of excitement being there. She followed Joshua up the stairs to the VIP sections to section one. Joshua had told Savannah that his brother Mark was part owner of the club and they were going to hang out with him. What she didn't know was that Joshua was also Mark's silent partner; a detail he hardly shared with anyone.

Savannah was taken aback by how handsome Mark was. Mark's smile and attentiveness to Joshua's introduction of Savannah let her know he'd felt the same. Mark blushed as he took her hand and kissed it; a gesture not made toward Jamya or Jalyssa. Sapphire noticed as well and was not happy about it.

"Nice to meet you Savannah," Mark said after finally finding the words to verbalize. "My brother spoke highly of you and your beauty but he by no means did you any justice."

Savannah smiled like a school girl and replied with a bashful "thank you".

"Please ladies have a seat," Mark said gesturing to the chairs. "And Sebastian," he added with a pat on Sebastian's shoulder.

Joshua and Mark introduced their groups to each other. Everyone was cordial except for Sapphire. Savannah picked up on her vibe and made a mental note to keep an eye on her. Savannah did not do female drama and didn't plan on starting that night. She spent the majority of the time focusing on the music in between engaging in some of the conversation. Savannah had a glass of Belair Rose´ that went to her head as well as her bladder.

"Excuse me Mark. Where's the restroom?" she asked.

"There's one down the stairs to the right. Need me to show you?"

"No, I think I'm good," Savannah replied.

"I have to go too so I'll go with you," Jamya said.

Jamya really didn't have to go but she felt the sexual aura Mark had put out toward Savannah and didn't want any problems. Savannah and Jamya made their way through the crowd to the bathroom. Savannah went into a bathroom stall while Jamya reapplied her lipstick.

"Thank you for coming with me," Savannah said when she came out of the stall.

"No problem. Mark was real interested in showing you himself though."

Savannah laughed, "Yeah. He's fine as hell though; he can show me anywhere he wants."

"Yeah, he is a cutie. I'm not sure exactly what's going on but I know there is some type of relationship between him and Sapphire just so you know."

"I figured something was up. I couldn't figure out if it

was because she was uppity or if it had something to do with Mark. It's cool. I'll let that be because I have a low tolerance for bullshit."

"I feel you there," Jamya said as they walked out of the bathroom.

They'd made it to the stairs when Savannah was grabbed by the hand. "What the hell?" she said as she turned to see who had grabbed her.

"Excuse me," he said.

"Yes, excuse you," she said snatching her hand.

"Can I speak to you for a second?"

Savannah didn't like being grabbed but she figured he was cute enough to at least hear him out. Jamya realized that Savannah wasn't behind her and turned around. Savannah waved her on and said she'd be right there.

"So how can I help you…"

"Emerick. Emerick Jeffries."

"Oh. You're the guy that got the birthday shout out."

"Yes I am," Emerick said smiling.

"Well happy birthday. So once again how can I help you?"

"First you can help me by giving me your name."

"Liza."

"Well Liza I think you're fine as hell and would love to

get to know you."

"Oh yeah?" Savannah said with a laugh. She could tell Emerick was the player type and wanted to get to know her alright; naked with his face buried in her boobs and/or pussy. *Thank you but no thank you.* "Listen Emerick thank you but I'm not interested. I hope you have a wonderful birthday," Savannah said leaving Emerick standing there.

"Bitch," he said to himself and he moved along to the next woman he had in his sights.

****

When Jamya got back to the VIP section without Savannah, Joshua asked about her.

"She stopped to talk to some guy by the stairs. She'll be up shortly," Jamya said.

Mark's eyes perked up at that statement. "Sapphire I'll be right back, I have to go check on something."

"Mark I'm not stupid. That Savannah girl is the 'something' you have to go check on."

"Sapphire don't start that shit. We have a great arrangement. Let's keep it that way. Stay in your place if you like the perks of your position," Mark said as he got up.

Jamya was ease dropping on their conversation. *Arrangement? Place? Position? I need to find out what's really going on.*

Diamond went to comfort her pouting sister. "Are you

okay Sapph?"

"How dare he talk to me like that? We've been doing this for a while and I'm not letting no country bunking big tittie bitch come between me and my paycheck," Sapphire said through flaring nostrils.

Jamya locked eyes with Jalyssa to see if she was hearing the conversation as well. She shook her head and they looked at each other crazy as Sapphire got up and went after Mark. *Ah hell,* Jamya thought; especially because Bubbles heard Sapphire as well and got up too. The street in Jamya wasn't going to let her new found dainty friend be in a situation to get jumped; plus she was their ride.

****

Savannah had just walked off from Emerick when Mark appeared.

"Are you alright?" he asked mean mugging Emerick.

"Yes," Savannah said.

Mark grabbed her by her waist and pulled her in a protective manner. Though Savannah had not been nervous or worried about Emerick, Mark brought a calming feeling to her as he closed the distance between them.

"Good. Even though my club is far from a hole in the wall, high class rift raft still get in from time to time," he said looking in Emerick's direction.

They'd just made it up the stairs when Sapphire came stumping their way. *Oh boy. This bougie bitch,* Savannah thought getting annoyed.

"Excuse me Mark but there are more important things that need your attention at this time," Sapphire said snidely.

"Not now Sapphire," he said turning his attention back to Savannah.

"I know you are not going to do me like that over some fake boob having skank."

"Skank?" Savannah started before she reminded herself that Sapphire wasn't worth her energy.

"Sapphire that is not called for. Act like a lady," Mark said.

Bubbles interjected before he could continue.

"Nah bitch. Who you calling a skank you fake ass Pageant Barbie wanna be. I will skull drag your prissy ass across this floor."

"Nobody is skull dragging nobody across the floor. So you might as well go somewhere with that thought," Jamya said standing toe to toe with Bubbles. "And before you act on any thought that might be rolling around in that mind, just know that I'm not as prissy as Sapphire here."

Jalyssa walked up at that time and Savannah felt it could get bad.

"Chill Bubbles, it's not even worth it. Let it go," Savannah said as she grabbed Bubble's arm and moved back to their area. Mark shook his head at Sapphire and followed Savannah and Bubbles.

****

"Are you alright?" Jamya asked Sapphire.

"Yes. I don't know what came over me. I never act like that. Thank you for having my back," she said with a forced smile.

"That's what friends do. Even new ones. Lets get out of here," Jamya said.

Sapphire gave her a genuine smile for the first time since they'd met. *Got her! She'll have to let me in on the hustle now,* she thought as Jalyssa went and got Diamond.

CHAPTER 8
About Last Night

Emerick woke with a headache from the pits of hell. He laid in the bed with his eyes closed hoping that some of the pressure he felt would subside. *Damn, I must have really got fucked up. I don't even remember leaving the club.* Emerick slowly opened his eyes and realized that he was not in his bedroom. He looked around and saw that he was in a hotel room; at Embassy Blasque. *What the hell?* he thought as he rubbed his head trying to remember the night before.

Emerick turned to his right when he heard a noise come from a room he assumed to be the bathroom. A slight panic came over him because he did not know who was on the other side of the door as it began to open. Emerick was relieved to see is was the young lady who gave him the exotic lap dance the night before. *Damn she thick; ass, titties, and thighs. Glad it ain't no ugly bitch,* he thought as he looked at her naked body.

"Hey sleepy head," she said with a smile.

"Hey yourself," Emerick said realizing he didn't know her name. "What exactly happened last?" he asked.

"Other than some bomb sex, we did some drinking and partying."

"Damn," he said rubbing his temples. "I can't remember a thing."

"Hmmm…I guess I'll have to make you some coffee, maybe order some room service, and then give you a replay of last night."

"Sounds good to me."

"Good because I want your body to call out Shaniece after I'm gone."

Shaniece. At least I know her name, but it has to be some for real bomb sex to have me thinking about that shit like that.

Shaniece grabbed a robe that hung in the closet and went into the kitchenette area. Emerick heard her humming while she prepared the coffee.

Where the hell is Mike, Emerick wondered as he grabbed his pants from beside the bed. He got his phone and texted Mike.

"Where are you?"

Emerick then checked for his wallet as well as his jewelry to make sure Shaniece didn't have happy fingers. He was glad to see that everything was there so he could tap that ass versus wanting to beat it. *Glad she's not one of those sorry tricks that be jacking brothers. Can't stand a thieving hoe.*

Emerick's phone went off; Mike had texted him back.

"I'm in the adjoining room with this fine honey. You good? Hope Shaniece served you up good."

"I can't remember. Lol. But she said she wants to give me a replay of last night."

"That's what's up. Check out is twelve so work that shit."

Shaniece came back into the room with the cup of coffee. "I hope it's sweet enough because there were only four packets of sugar."

"Thank you," Emerick said as he sat up in the bed.

"So do you want something to eat?"

"Nah, I think everything I need is in this room."

"Oh yeah?" Shaniece asked playfully.

Emerick took a slow sip of the coffee and nodded his head yes.

"Well I'm going to hop in the shower on that note," she said with a wink.

Emerick continued to sip the coffee praying that it would help his head. He was glad Mike knew enough to bring him to Embassy Blasque. Embassy Blasque had been where he usually laid his head after nights of partying. He'd taken several women there as well. The number was few because he'd get cheaper hotel rooms for the ones not worthy of anything other than getting dicked down. Emerick prided himself on his ability to please a woman and he was determined to do Shaniece that favor. Because of his frequent visits to the hotel he knew they carried aspirin so he called down to the front desk.

"Front desk. Can I help you?"

"Yes. I need a pack of aspirin please."

"No problem. I'll send someone with it shortly. Anything else sir?"

"No, that will be all. Thank you."

"You're very welcome and thank you for visiting us at Embassy Blasque."

Emerick sipped more of his coffee. He felt it was helping with his head but in actuality that thought was only in his mind; encouraged by his pulsating penis and growing sexual desire.

Emerick heard a knock at the door so he grabbed his boxers from the floor and put them on. When Emerick opened the door the hotel attendant handed him the aspirin. Emerick said thank you and noticed the young man checking him out as he closed the door. *Oh hell no. I don't even go that way bruh,* he thought after he closed the door completely and moved to the kitchenette for water.

Shaniece finished her shower and stood there and watched Emerick as he took the pills. When he put the glass down on the counter she walked behind him and embraced him.

"Oh," Emerick said startled by her action.

"Sorry daddy. Didn't mean to scare you. You looked so good. Got me wanting you," she said stroking his penis through his boxers. "Can I give him a good morning kiss? Pleeeease," she purred in his ear.

"I think he'd like that."

Emerick turned around and Shaniece pulled his boxers down. She pushed Emerick to the counter, squatted down, and put him in her mouth. *Damn, she works that mouth like a suction cup,* he thought. Emerick watched her and admired the water droplets on her back and her heart shaped ass. Shaniece worked Emerick so good he was moaning like he never had before. It messed him up at first and he fought the urge until finally he was like fuck it and gave into Shaniece's pleasure. His headache had subsided and he was ready to get up in Shaniece's goodies.

"Dang girl, you're going to make me nut," Emerick said slightly over a whisper.

Shaniece looked at him giving him a suck and tongue rub. Emerick's responses to her touch turned Shaniece on. Her juices were flowing and she was ready to feel him. Shaniece released Emerick's fully erected penis from the warmth of her mouth. She laid kisses on his balls, up his shaft, to his head, up his stomach, up his chest, and all the way to his lips. They were wrapped in a passionate kiss when Emerick turned her around and put her hands on the counter top. He got on his knees, spread her legs, and dove into her honey pot of goodness. Shaniece shrilled in pleasure from the attention Emerick was showing her; he sucked, licked, and kissed his way to the root of her wetness. Shaniece gripped the counter top for stability as her legs shook from the orgasmic eruption that was happening within her body. The more pleasure Shaniece displayed, the more Emerick put into his pleasing.

"Ah shit Emerick. I can't take no more. Give it to me please," Shaniece begged.

Those words made pre-cum ooze from his rock hard penis. He had another plan for her before he gave her the dick though. Emerick cupped her cheeks and dove into her ass. "Damn," Shaniece said as he worked her second hole. She yearned to feel Emerick inside of her as she dripped wetness from both holes.

Emerick continued to tease her until he got to the point where he couldn't deny his throbbing desire anymore. He got up and placed his head on Shaniece's vagina lips. Shaniece braced herself for the initial thrust. When it didn't happen, she turned around and asked, "What's wrong?"

"I have to go get a condom. Play with it until I go grab my

wallet."

Though Emerick got caught slipping quite a few times, after the Jade and baby ordeal he attempted to be more responsible. Emerick ran and got the condom. He walked back to Shaniece and smiled at her obedience.

"You got her ready for me?" he asked as he opened the condom.

"Yes. She's ready," she said seductively.

Emerick bent her back over the counter and entered her from behind. *Damn that pussy's warm. She feels as good as she tasted.* Emerick went in and out of her with a steady rhythm. His eight and a half inch thick rod was a pleaser, but the drunk sex they had the night before did not hold a candle to the sex Emerick was giving her at that moment. *Yeah, that dick got her going crazy,* he thought going deeper inside of her. She screamed as he hit her "G" spot. Shaniece let out a screech and squirted on Emerick. He slow grinded her as she had three orgasms back to back. Emerick pulled out and lead her to the bed.

He let her catch her breath as he ate her out once again. Emerick enjoyed to watch Shaniece. He felt something different with her than he did with the other sexual encounters; he couldn't put his finger on what it was or why. They moved around the entire king sized bed until they ended their episode with Shaniece on top Emerick riding him like a cowgirl. *She might be right. My body just might be calling her name later,* he thought as he exploded in the condom.

****

Jamya and Jalyssa ended up sleeping on Diamond and Sapphire's sofa and love seat. After the club they'd gone back to the apartment, drunk wine, and talked. Most of the conversation was girl talk type of talk but the most interesting thing was Diamond and Sapphire sharing about their hustle. Jamya found out that they found sponsors to take care of them.

"So y'all like some escorts or something?" Jalyssa had asked.

"No. We're what you call sugar babies," Sapphire said.

"Sugar babies?" Jamya asked with a confused look on her face.

"Yeah. We seek out sugar daddies to take care of us," Diamond nonchalantly said.

"Shit like that really happen?" Jalyssa asked.

"Look around and you tell me," Sapphire said waving her arm around the apartment.

"That's what's up," Jalyssa said pouring another glass of *Belaire Rose.*

"We started at cons," Sapphire said.

"Yeah, we watched that movie 'Heartbreakers' about the woman and her daughter running cons on men. That's where we got the idea," Diamond interjected.

"Yeah, we did well enough to live but then we found out about the sugar baby craze and it has elevated our living," Sapphire continued.

"Wow," was all Jamya could say while her brain was fast at work. They finished four bottles of wine and crashed.

****

Savannah sat on the plane replaying her California visit; the photo shoot, Club Night Life, and Mark. They stayed at the club for about an hour after the Sapphire incident. Mark showed her lots of attention and she liked ever moment of it.

They exchanged numbers before she left. She woke to a *"Good morning beautiful"* text and a *"Let me take you to brunch before you leave"* text. Savannah took Mark up on his offer. He took her to a restaurant overlooking the LA River. They'd spent the entire time prior to her three o'clock flight together.

Thinking back to the conversation and laughs they shared, Savannah blushed on the plane. Mark sent her off with flowers and a kiss that had Savannah eager to return to Los Angeles.

Emily was waiting for Savannah when she got off of the plane.

"You looking all LA and refreshed," Emily said once Savannah got into the car.

"Well…you know," Savannah said playfully.

"Bitch you cheesing real hard over there. Spill it."

"Well I told you the photo shoot was nice and the girls were cool as shit but I met someone."

"Met someone? Oh hell," Emily said rolling her eyes.

"Whatever. His name's Mark. He owns a club. He seems pretty alright but time will tell."

"Just be careful."

"I will. So what did I miss while I was gone?"

"You ain't missed shit. Them hoes at the club still stupid as hell."

Savannah laughed. "Some things will never change. I had a good time in LA but there's no place like home."

CHAPTER 9
Guess Who's Coming To Dinner

Emerick and Shaniece got quite close after his birthday. For the first time in his life he was only with one woman sexually. They did not have an official relationship but they had an understanding that worked well for the both of them. Though it worked for them, Emerick knew it would not work for his mother. She would say that Shaniece was not fit to be the woman let alone the wife of her son, the heir of Diamont Brut. Shaniece was a dancer at a gentleman's club in Beverly Hills.

Emerick knew that even with the upscale nature in which she worked, Shaniece would be looked upon as a slutty money hungry stripper to his mother. However, Emerick however, did not care about Shaniece being a stripper because she was more than a pretty face and fat ass. Shaniece had been the realest woman he'd ran across. He also liked that she was a well diverse woman. They could talk about anything from ass to politics to philosophy. Shaniece didn't strip because she couldn't do anything else but because she enjoyed doing it and did not care what anyone said. That trait alone appealed to Emerick because his whole life he had to worry about what his mother said and how she felt about a situation.

Emerick and Shaniece spent their time together at hotels, at her condo, or traveling. Things were going great and before Emerick knew it, it had been a year of them "kicking" it. Their chill was disrupted when Mary Ann approached him about the relationship. He knew something was up because she came to his room; something she never did. When she wanted something she normally used the intercom system.

"Come in," Emerick said when he heard the knock on the door.

"Emerick."

"Mother. What's wrong?" he responded confused by her presence.

"Nothing. Can't a woman come speak to her son?"

Woman...yes. You...no.

"Of course."

"Good," she said as she sat on his bed. "It's really nice in here," she continued as she looked around.

"Thanks Mother but what's on your mind?"

"So tell me about this young lady you are seeing."

"What young lady?"

"The one you're always talking to and sneaking off with.

I'm not blind Emerick, so tell me."

"There's not much to tell. Her name is Shaniece and she's really nice."

"So when will I get to meet her?"

"Oh no. We're not ready for that yet."

"Well get ready. Invite her to come to dinner tomorrow."

"Tomorrow? But-"

"There's no but. I need to check this young lady out. We cannot have you wasting your time on someone not worthy of our last name."

"But-"

"There you go with the buts again. Make it happen," she said and then left his room.

"Shit," Emerick said. Then he had a bright idea to just prep Shaniece to fit into his mother's ideal image of a wife.

****

Against Shaniece's better judgment she agreed to go to dinner at Emerick's. She tried hard to avoid any type of family interaction. She had a huge secret that she wanted to let remain a secret. She hung up the phone with Emerick and immediately made another call.

"Thank you for calling Diamont Brut, this is Melissa. How can I help you?" the receptionist said.

"Mr. Allen Jeffries please."

"Who may I say is calling please?"

"Let him know it's Niecey," Shaniece responded.

The receptionist put her on a brief hold before Allen picked up.

"Hello."

"Hey Allen it's Niecey.

"I haven't spoken to you in a while. What's up sweetness?" he asked through a big smile.

"We have a big problem."

"What type of problem?" he asked sounding alarmed.

"Your wife has requested my presence at your house."

"What? My wife? When? Why?"

"I've been seeing your son off and on over the last year."

"That's cold Niecey. How are you going to do a thing like that?"

"First off let's be honest, there was never anything between us other than your lust for me. I was just the latest fuck from the club. At first I didn't know he was your son, but once I did it was too late and the shit was too good to let it go. I'm sorry Allen but I need for you to not tell Emerick about us. I really like him and don't want to ruin the relationship we have. I'm begging you," she pleaded.

Allen sat behind his desk and rubbed the thinning spot

on the top of his head. He took a deep breath taking in what Shaniece had said before he responded with, "Alright."

"Thank you Allen. I will see you tomorrow," she said and then hung up the phone.

CHAPTER 10
Latin Sugar

"How do I look?" Jalyssa asked Jamya.

She looked at Jalyssa in a black and grey Bebe dress and wedge heels. "You look hot as usual. What are you about to get into?"

"Mike called me and we're going to hang out for a bit. Grab some dinner and chill at his place for awhile before I'm his dessert," she said with a wink.

"Well at least y'all are going out to eat this time."

"Shit, the way he lays that dick down that motherfucker ain't got to do nothing else but that!"

"You are hell!" Jamya exclaimed and laughed.

"For real though. That shit be having me weak," Jalyssa said staring into space.

"Damn girl, don't get caught up and don't give him the super head. We have business to handle and it don't include a sprung brother up your ass."

"You don't have to worry about that. You know I'm about that paper," Jamya said matter-a-factly.

"Good. Hope you have fun."

"Ha! I am. Can't wait to climb that six foot four inch tree," Jalyssa said rolling her hips and humping the air.

They both laughed as Jalyssa left out of Jamya's room. Jamya got out of her comfortable pillow top bed and went to her closet; a closet that was filled with beautiful designer clothes. Things had been going great for the girls after Diamond and Sapphire turned them onto the sugar baby scene. They'd created profiles on a sugar baby website and immediately were approached by men wanting a pretty young thing to spoil. It blew them how easy it was, but they were happy the dollars were flowing in. Their apartment was no longer bare and their bank accounts and stashed money both stayed full.

Jamya had a date that day with Francesco Sandoval. Francesco was her handsome middle aged Latin lover. Francesco was a retired model and Latin actor. In addition to being a part time sugar baby, Jamya also persuaded a hidden love of art by getting a job as a gallery assistant at a downtown art gallery. She met Francesco at the gallery opening. She almost passed out when the William Levy with salt and pepper hair looking man approached her looking sexy in an all black Armani suit accessorized with a beautiful smile. He intrigued her and in turn he'd been the main guy in her life for a little over six months. Though he did provide her with money and expensive gifts she made sure to never put him in the sugar daddy category.

Francesco introduced her to a new and more luxurious lifestyle. Their dates included yacht rides, upscale dinners, romantic weekend getaways, and movie premiers. That day they were going to a wine tasting at the Hillcrest Country Club.

Jamya stood in the closet overwhelmed by all of the possible outfits in her closet. After what seemed like forever she settled on a strapless black jumpsuit and black, white, and royal blue swirled pumps. She laid her outfit on the bed and went for her jewelry box to lay out her accessories when she heard Jalyssa yell, "I'm leaving Mya."

"Okay honey. See you later," Jamya yelled back before hearing their front door close.

Jamya continued getting ready for her date. After finding what she felt was the perfect accessories for her outfit she showered and got dressed. There was a knock on the apartment door as she put on her second shoe.

"Who is it?" she asked as she walked to the door.

"It's Sapphire," Sapphire said from the other side of the door.

"Hey girl," Jamya said when she opened the door.

"Damn," Sapphire said when she say Jamya. "Looking

good mama. Came to see what you were up to but the better question is who you're up to!"

"Girl, stop. This old thing," Jamya said playfully.

Sapphire laughed, "Yes. That OLD thing."

Sapphire and Jamya had gotten close after their bonding moment in Club Night Life. Jamya quickly realized the snobby stuck up personality was only Sapphire's defense mechanism to protect her true vulnerability. Though Sapphire never shared her past with Jamya, she had a feeling that Sapphire had been in some type of foul situation. Jamya ran across a lot of females like Sapphire back in Chicago.

"So what's up?" Jamya asked as they walked into her bedroom.

"Ain't nothing really. Diamond is going out tonight with her friend Hilary. I can't get with that valley girl shit they're into so I'm just relaxing at home this evening. Plus Mark is going to Vegas on some club business so I don't want to go to the club. So where are you off too? Looking fabulous I must say."

"I'm going to a wine tasting at Hillcrest with Francesco."

"That sounds fun."

"It's my first time going to one so I'm pretty excited."

"Don't forget it's a tasting because it's too easy to get drunk at one of those things. Want me to do your make up?"

"Sure."

She finished getting ready with Sapphire's help and Francesco came about thirty minutes later to whisk her off. Jamya left looking forward to an enjoyable evening, not knowing she was going to have to take the same advise she had given Jalyssa before she left.

Jamya spent the night with Francesco. They had gotten a room at the country club after the tasting. She enjoyed the resort getaway feel of the country club. Though she and Francesco had a good time that evening, Jamya felt as if he had been distant.

"Francesco baby what's wrong? It seems like something has been on your mind."

Francesco gave her a faint smile, "Come sit down my beauty," he said ushering her to the sitting area. Jamya sat and he placed his hand on her knee. "I have not been completely forth coming with you and now I must." Jamya did not know nor like what was going to come out of his mouth next. That statement and the tone he used was a lot heavier than he'd usually used with her. Looking Jamya in her eyes Francesco continued, "I told you that my family is in El Salvador but what I did not tell you is that my family includes a wife and two small children." Jamya was crushed but she refused to express that emotion as she sat there. "My wife Isabel wants to come to California now." Francesco grabbed Jamya's hand, "I do not want to lose you Jamya. You've brought great happiness to me these last months."

Jamya's advice to Jalyssa surfaced to her mind. She swallowed her emotions and responded, "Francesco honey I will forgive you for your secret this time, but know it will cost you."

He smiled, "Anything for you darling. Just name it."

Being the other woman will not be so bad. I'll get the dick, time, and gifts without the bullshit. That ass will pay for hurting my feelings though.

"Don't worry I will cash in later but for now come here and let mama spank you for being bad."

Francesco's smile widened and he allowed Jamya to dominate him throughout the night.

CHAPTER 11
What Happens In Vegas

Things for Savannah changed after her visit to Los Angeles. She'd gotten several jobs after her spread in Passion House was released. Savannah went from a small town girl to a girl traveling to places such as LA, Miami, and Dallas. Because of all the gigs she was doing Savannah only worked at the club part time. For the first time in her life she felt like she was living.

Savannah and Mark continued their communication after she returned home. Their relationship progressed quickly. Besides their phone calls and text messages throughout the day they'd each made several trips to see each other. By six months Savannah had met Mark's mother Julia and Mark had met Royce.

Savannah felt like she was winning in her modeling career and in love. Many times she expected to wake up and realize she'd been dreaming. Lucky for her that had not happened though.

Savannah was in her room packing her suitcase when Royce came in.

"How's it going Baby Girl?"

"I'm good," Savannah replied with a huge smile on her face.

"It looks that way. I'm heading out for work so I wanted to come bid you a fare well," he said with a hug and forehead kiss.

"Thanks Pops."

"You have a fun and safe trip."

"I will."

"Not too much fun though. Don't make me a grandpa yet," he said with a chuckle.

"Oh Pops! Cut it out," Savannah said with a chuckle as well.

"Love you Baby Girl."

"Love you too Pops."

Royce left out of her room and Savannah continued packing.

She and Mark were going to Vegas. They were celebrating the anniversary of the night they met; as Mark put it, the night he fell in love. Mark had been secretive on the plans so she was excited to see what he had in stored for their four day visit.

Savannah finished packing her suitcase and headed to the airport in the Honda Civic she'd purchased. Emily called her on her way.

"Hey Em. What's up?"

"Nothing much. Just taking a break from some homework and wanted to talk to you before you leave cause I know Mark is gonna have that ass on lock when you touch down."

"Ha ha."

"Just saying," she said laughing. "Are you excited about going to Vegas?"

"Hell yeah."

"Don't get drunk and get married or no shit like that," Emily said still laughing.

"You ain't got to worry about that!"

"Uh huh. I don't know. You and mister been getting mighty close. But shit if you gonna do it you might as well do it with a guy like Mark. He's fine, sweet, and rich!"

"I'm not playing with you today Emily. You're a mess," Savannah said laughing.

"I ain't lying though."

"True."

"Well have a good time sis."

"Thanks Em. I'll call you when I get back. Love you!"

"Love you too!"

****

Savannah was greeted at baggage claim by a man holding a sign with her name on it. She smiled because she'd seen that on TV before and never thought things like that happened to regular people like her. "Good afternoon Ms. Biggs. I am Anthony and I will be driving you to the Bellagio. How many bags do you have ma'am?"

"Two."

"Point them out when they come on the conveyor belt and I will grab them," Anthony said to Savannah.

He led Savannah to a Lincoln Continental once they'd gotten her bags. She sat back and took in the sights as Anthony drove. He periodically gave her known facts of the places they passed.

"Wow," Savannah said softly as they pulled up in front of the hotel.

"Beautiful isn't is?" Anthony asked looking at the wide eyed Savannah.

"Absolutely beautiful," she said.

"Not as beautiful as you," Mark said behind Savannah.

"Hey baby!" Savannah exclaimed. She was so taken aback by the scenery she had not seen him until then. She hugged him around his neck and kissed him. The kiss was magical for Savannah. Though she'd fought it for awhile, Savannah had fallen head over heels in love with Mark. When she was with him, she had no worries.

"How was your flight?" he asked after they separated from their kiss.

"It was good. The airport was crazy! I wasn't expecting there to be a casino in it."

"Yeah, that got me the first time I came to Vegas too. I'm glad you're here," Mark said pulling Savannah close to him.

"Me too."

The bell hop got Savannah's bags and they went up to the suite Mark had reserved for their trip.

"Oh my goodness," Savannah said when she walked into the large suite. She bounced around the room, "This place is like an apartment. This is beautiful Mark. Thank you for bringing me here."

"Anything for you darling."

Savannah landed another passionate kiss on Mark that ended with them making love in the luxurious suite.

****

Savannah and Mark's trip to Las Vegas was coming to an end. She had enjoyed herself up to that point. "This is our last day, so what are we going to do today?" Savannah said as they cuddled in the bed.

"First, I'm thinking we order breakfast, an early morning

quickie, a couple's massage, an afternoon love making session, a show, and-"

"Let me guess, some more love making," Savannah said with a giggle.

"No. Dinner and then some more love making," he said laughing.

"Sounds good."

"The love making?"

"The whole plan silly."

"I can't get enough of you baby," Mark expressed with a kiss.

"Hmmm. Keep kissing me like that and the quickie may just come before breakfast," Savannah said playfully.

"That can be arranged as well beautiful."

"Oh yeah?"

"Yeah," Mark said before they started a hot and heavy session of kissing and rubbing.

Mark's phone began to ring as their tongues slow danced. He ignored it as they continued their hot and heavy transference of energy. The phone immediately rang again. Mark planted a soft kiss on Savannah's lips and said, "Let me get that. It may be important." He got the phone and said, "This is my club manager. Give me a second."

Savannah nodded her head as he walked off. Savannah

laid in the bed with the room service menu and waited for Mark to get done with his call.

****

Savannah was giddy her entire plane ride home. She could not wait to get back to Raleigh to talk to Emily. After getting her bag at baggage claim, Savannah rushed to her car. She immediately called Emily, "Em are you at home?" she asked before Emily could even say hello.

"Yeah. Welcome back superstar. What's going on?"

"I'm on my way over. I have something to show you."

"Okay, it better involve a really cool gift for your best friend."

"Of course," Savannah said with a soft chuckle. "I'll see you in a minute."

When Savannah arrived at Emily's apartment she went in her bag and got the gift bag she had for Emily. Savannah skipped up the stairs to Emily's apartment.

"You're real chipper today. Mark must have out done himself this time."

"He sure did," Savannah said waving her hand.

"Holy hell! Is that an engagement ring?" Emily asked grabbing Savannah's hand to look at the one and a half carat princess cut diamond ring with diamond incrusted band. "Eeekk," Emily squealed.

They sat on the couch and Savannah started telling Emily about the proposal. "Oh my god my trip was amazing; from the suite, to the shows, to the food, and definitely the pampering. He made me feel like a queen…" Savannah said as she daydreamed.

"Alright already. Tell me."

"Oh. Well it was yesterday morning. We were getting all hot and heavy when his club manager called and interrupted. When he got off the phone, he told me to go shower while he ordered us breakfast. I actually decided to take a bath to try out the whirlpool tub; which was amazing I must add. Anyways, when I was done Mark was waiting at the table with the covered trays. I sat down and he goes into telling me how much he loves me and how I've changed his life. Well, when I took the cover off of my tray I was surprised to see a ring box. It was opened showcasing this beautiful ring. He gets it and gets on one knee. Mind you I'm speechless because in my mind I'm like I know this isn't happening. He asked me to marry him and I said yes."

"Oh my god! That is beautiful. I'm happy for you and glad you didn't go to some chapel and let Elvis marry you."

Savannah began laughing and Emily added, "You didn't did you?"

"Of course not. I can't dream of having a wedding

without you or Pops there. He did mention us getting married there."

"He's trying to hurry up and lock you down! I'm glad you thought about us though. Love you girl!"

"Love you too Em!"

CHAPTER 12
To Be Or Not To Be

"Emerick baby, I can drive myself," Shaniece said through the phone.

"Yes, but I'd rather pick you up. We can go over our story."

"We've gone over our story enough. I got it, I run my own internet business."

"What type?"

Trying to fight her agitation she replied, "A clothing boutique."

"Named?"

"Look Emerick, I got the damn story. I'm sorry to snap at you but either your mother is going to like me or not. It's that simple."

"I know I've been riding you about this dinner Shaniece but I want my mother to see you the way I do. I want her to give you a fair shot without the hang ups of what you do. I'm sorry. If you'd like to drive that's fine."

"Thank you Emerick. I will see you in a few."

"Okay," Emerick said.

Emerick wasn't the only one worried about the evening; Shaniece and Allen both shared his anxiety.

Emerick met Shaniece when she pulled up to their home. He opened her door and instantly smiled at her outfit selection.

"You look great baby," Emerick said with a kiss. Shaniece looked sleek in the black high waisted slacks, black and white polka dotted blouse, and black and white pumps.

"Thank you love. I'm glad you approve," she replied slickly.

Emerick choose not to respond because he knew he deserved it after his behavior. He just smiled and offered his arm. "This way my lady." Shaniece returned the smile and grabbed his arm

They were greeted by Amyra at the door. "Good evening ma'am. Welcome to the Jefferies residence."

"Thank you very much," Shaniece replied as she took in the elegant decor.

"Mister Jefferies the Madame said that she would be down shortly and for you to show your friend the grounds."

Emerick nodded and lead Shaniece through the house to the back door. They strolled through the garden ending at a fountain.

"This is beautiful," Shaniece said. "I would spend most if

not all of my time out here."

"Actually I don't remember the last time I've come out here."

"You got to be kidding me! It's the small things you have to start appreciating darling. Money is great but it is not everything love," she said flicking some of the water at Emerick.

He laughed at the unexpected gesture. Those were the things that he enjoyed about his and Shaniece's relationship. He hugged her, "Thank you for being such a good friend Shaniece." He kissed her on the forehead and said, "Let's make our way back to the house."

They were talking and laughing when they walked in, not noticing Mary Ann in the sitting room. "Uh hum," she said.

Startled Emerick said, "Oh Mother I didn't see you there."

"Obviously."

Shaniece didn't like the vibe she got from Mary Ann but brushed it off because she had heard she was a bitch.

"Mother this is Shaniece. Shaniece this is my mother Mary Ann Jeffries."

"Nice to meet you," Shaniece said stretching her hand out.

"Likewise," Mary Ann said looking down at her

extended hand.

"Okay," Shaniece said under her breath as she pulled her lonely hand back.

Lord let me get through this evening with both my mother and my girl speaking to me, Emerick thought. "Where's Dad?" Emerick asked filling the awkward silence.

"He should be down momentarily. He was putting on his tie for this special occasion."

"Madame the table is set," Amyra said.

"Thank you Amyra. Emerick show your friend to the dining room. I will fetch your father."

Emerick and Shaniece began to move toward the dining room when Allen meet them in the door way.

"I hope I didn't miss any fun," he said sensing that Mary Ann's horns were out. "Hello, I'm Allen," he continued extending his hand.

"I'm Shaniece."

"Nice to meet you," he said after their brief hand shake. "Were you all moving to the dining room?"

"Yes dear," Mary Ann said through a forced smile.

Dinner went as well as Emerick could expect with his mother's over bearing personality.

"So, Shaniece is it?"

"Yes ma'am."

"My Emerick seems to be quite fond of you."

Shaniece smiled and replied, "And I am fond of him as well," while looking at Emerick.

"So how did you two meet? Seeing as Emerick has been so secretive."

Emerick tensed as he wondered how Shaniece would spin that they met at a club and ended the night with him drunk fucking her.

"Actually we met by way of some mutual acquaintances a little over a year ago and then we got reacquainted on his birthday."

Good girl! Nicely put, he thought as he felt a feeling of relief sweep over him.

"We've been talking and seeing one another since then.

"That sounds really nice," Mary Ann stated with a half smile.

"Yes it does," Allen interjected.

"What is it that you do?" Mary Ann asked Shaniece.

"I have an online boutique."

"Interesting."

"Yes, it has been an interesting yet enjoyable process." Mary Ann nodded her head as Shaniece continued with her well rehearsed lie.

When Amyra came in with dessert Emerick began to

breathe easy because they made it through dinner. *It's almost over. Thank you Jesus,* Emerick thought. Unfortunately, Emerick's thoughts were interrupted when his mother made the statement, "It's funny how you sit there acting so civilized when you are no more than a slut."

"Excuse me?" Shaniece said.

"You heard me you slut."

"Emerick, I am leaving. I will not be disrespected by your mother," Shaniece said scooting her chair back.

"Mother! You apologize to Shaniece," Emerick exclaimed.

"I will not do no such thing. Let her trashy ass leave."

"Mary Ann that is enough," Allen interjected.

"Why because she is one of your whores?"

A hush moved through the room. "What?" Emerick finally had the strength to muster up.

"I'm sorry son but your father is not the squeaky clean man he portrays. He has a love for young girls with big asses; Shaniece being one." Shaniece grabbed her purse and moved toward the door with Emerick on her heel. Mary Ann turned to Allen, "My father's legacy is too important to me to not protect it. I'm sick and tired of your ignorance. I've kept very close tabs on you darling. I've been giving you enough rope to hang yourself, and you've succeeded."

Emerick's heart was hurt. "How could you?" he asked when they reached Shaniece's car.

"It's not what it looks like Emerick. Please let me explain."

"Explain what? That you've been fucking my father?"

"I've not been with Allen since I met you. I did not know he was your father at first and when I put two and two together I'd already caught feelings for you. I was afraid to tell you. I thought it could have been just another mistake in my list of many."

"My dad though Shaniece."

"I'm truly sorry Emerick. I hope we can still be friends."

"Friends don't keep secrets that can hurt their friends. Drive safe Shaniece," Emerick said as he walked away.

Emerick went into the house, got his keys, and went out to get wasted.

****

The days after the explosive dinner party had Emerick on edge. He had not spoken to Shaniece even as badly as he wanted to, his father stayed at the downtown condo that Diamont Brut owned, and he was just plain angry.

Emerick was out by the pool having a drink when his mother joined him.

"Emerick."

"Mother," he replied without looking at her.

"I need to speak to you son," she said taking a seat next to him.

"I'm listening," Emerick said coldly.

"Look at me please son."

He looked up at her and she continued, "My intent is never to hurt you, but in my attempts to protect you, sometimes I do. I'm truly sorry son."

Emerick had not heard his mother speak in such a tender tone since he was a small boy, but his anger would not allow her to get off the hook that easy. "But why Mother? You set this whole thing up from the beginning to expose her."

"Yes, there are not many things that I leave up to chance. Especially when it comes to my family. Emerick you are my son and we do not take the words of others. So I figured bringing it to the fore front would be the only way you would believe it. I know you're hurt son, but I need for you to pull yourself out of this funk. It is time for you to take your rightful place at Diamont Brut."

"Mother I'm not ready to-"

"Son you HAVE to get ready. I'm going to be frank with you. Your father and I have been having problems for many years now; hence his many affairs. There is a huge chance that our time together is coming to an end."

"You don't know that Mother."

"Yes I do Emerick," Mary Ann said sadly. "We have to protect the family business."

"Okay Mother."

"Remember things aren't always what they seem son." Mary Ann gave Emerick a hug and left him to his drink.

CHAPTER 13
Things Aren't Always As They Seem

"Man this is nice," Jalyssa said looking at Jamya's new car; a silver convertible Chevrolet Camaro with chrome rims.

Jamya had been planning on getting a vehicle but was not in a rush because there were tons of transportation options in LA. Once Francesco opened himself up for his debt, Jamya cashed in with the car.

"I love it!" Jalyssa said.

"Get in."

Jalyssa jumped in with no hesitation. "All black interior…sunroof…GPS…blue tooth…satellite radio. Damn Mya you got all the bells and whistles. You must of really put it on Francesco's ass!"

"Well, you know how I do!" The girls laughed. "Let's let the top down and go shopping."

"Shit let's go then," Jalyssa said.

Jamya put on Rihanna's *Bitch Better Have My Money*. "This song is dedicated to Francesco and his sweet Isabel," she said and peeled out of the parking lot.

The girl's shopping trip was cut short when Jamya's boss

117

Sahara called, "Jamya darling I need for you to please come in and help me with tonight's showing. George has fell ill. I know it is short notice and for that I will double your wages for today."

Jamya didn't need the double pay so that didn't appeal to her but she did love the new artist showcases. "I am out right now but I can be there in an hour and half. Is that good?"

"That is wonderful. Thank you Jamya."

"You're welcome Sahara. See you then."

When Jamya and Jalyssa got back to their apartment Jamya began getting herself ready for work. She pulled out a garment bag and filled it with the outfit she would change into for the actual showcase; a little black dress, attention grabbing pumps, dangling pearl earrings, and a pearl and diamond accented bracelet. Jamya then showered, put on some yoga pants and a shirt, and did her hair and makeup.

"I'm out Jalyssa. Hit me up if you decide you want to go out scouting tonight," Jamya shouted at Jalyssa on her way out.

"Okay mama. Have a good day at work."

****

"Yo bro what you getting into tonight?"

"Man, my mom has me going to this art gallery tonight for some new pieces for the office. I'm not feeling it either. We have people who could do that but she is insisting that I go personally," Emerick said to Mike over the phone.

"Man bro, I don't even know why you are tripping. You know that's how your mama is. Just remember that it could be a heck of a lot worst errand."

"True. I don't know why the things she do still surprise me."

"I don't either. So how's things been going? You talk to your pops yet?"

"Nah. It's been going is all I can say. I miss the shit out of Shaniece. Not the sex either, just her."

"Damn bro. Why don't you hit her up?"

"Because she was not fucking a homeboy or an acquaintance but my pops. That's a little much to swallow. At least right now."

"I feel you with that though. You'll be alright bro. You'll get through this like everything else. Plus you are the President at a multimillion dollar company. Pussy is constantly being thrown at you! Holler at me after your art thing."

"Alright man. Thanks for the pep talk."

"Always."

****

Jamya was finally done with all the preparations for the showcase. She ran around for hours ensuring that the stagers placed each piece in the correct places with the correct lighting. Jamya got into beast mode whenever she was dealing with the exhibits; Sahara had no worries when she was on the job. Jamya did one more walk through and then changed into her event outfit.

"You look stunning as usual," Sahara complimented her when she returned from the restroom. Sahara really liked Jamya but she worried that she was like so many of the young women who came to LA for the glitz and glimmer. She noticed Jamya's expensive taste and assumed she lived above her means; not knowing in actuality Jamya's bank account was stacked more than hers.

"Thank you Sahara. You look beautiful as well."

"Thank you darling. Are you ready for another milestone in the Art of Art's history?"

"Of course. Let's work our magic."

Jamya and Sahara worked the room the entire evening peaking interest in everyone who gave them their ear. The showing was going well; pieces were sold and the guest were all mingling pleasantly.

Jamya was engaged in a conversation with a local artist when Emerick entered the gallery. He caught her eye in her peripheral vision. When he moved into her clear sight she thought *he looks familiar.* She admired the confidence he showed as he strolled across the floor. After a few minutes she suppressed that annoying feeling of trying to place the familiarity of his face. Jamya finished her conversation and then moved on toward her mission of ensuring h'orderves were moving around the room as they should when Sahara approached her with Emerick.

"Jamya I have someone for you to meet. This is Emerick Jeffries he..." Jamya didn't hear what Sahara said after that because she was trying to figure out where she'd heard that name before.

"Nice to meet you Jamya," Emerick said with a hand shake.

"Likewise."

"Jamya is quite knowledgeable and she will make sure that you are taken care of," Sahara said.

"Thank you very much," Jamya replied.

Sahara shot both of them a smile before she moved along. She walked off with a smirk on her face because she noticed the way Emerick looked at Jamya; she could tell that Jamya intrigued him.

"Are you alright?" Emerick asked Jamya.

"Yes. I'm sorry. You look very familiar and I've been trying to figure out from where."

Emerick began naming possible places they may had met but Jamya said no to all of his suggestions. "Maybe I just have one of those faces," he added.

Hell no with your sexy ass! That is definitely not just "one of those" type of faces. "I don't think so. Onto business. Do you have an idea what you are looking for?"

"Something unique for my office space. Is this artist any good?"

"She's superb. Her name is Alana Sanchez. Follow me as I show you one of my favorite pieces in her collection." Jamya lead Emerick to an abstract piece.

"Hmmm. Nice," Emerick said nodding his head. "Why is this among your favorite?"

"I like the emotion behind it. First off she used warm earth tones that I love. The mixture of browns, red, and yellow are calming. I also appreciate the strength in her brush strokes," Emerick moved closer as Jamya continued, "The whirls are all calculated and not sporadic. I especially like this portion that swoops across the canvas. It reminds me of a soft breeze. I see peace when I look at this picture," Jamya said with a smile as she gazed at the picture.

"Amazing."

"Yes it is pretty amazing."

"I was actually talking about that you got all of that from this picture. I've never looked into a painting that in depth before but you've given me a new appreciation."

"I'm glad that I could do that for you," Jamya smiled hoping that a sale would follow.

"I would like for this 'peaceful' piece to be one of my selections. So now to your other favorites of the collection."

"Great. Let me tag this one with your number first to ensure no one steals it from under your nose." Jamya tagged the canvas and continued her journey around the gallery with Emerick.

The end of the evening brought Emerick purchasing three canvases, one sculpture, and Emerick and Jamya exchanging numbers.

Sahara was quite pleased with how the night turned out. "Jamya tonight was incredible. Alana's entire collection with the exception of four pieces was sold."

"That is pretty incredible."

"You're incredible Jamya."

"Oh quit it Sahara," Jamya said modestly.

"No seriously. The way you interact with the people is fascinating. You have the personality that has people ready to buy whatever you are selling," Sahara said with a grin. Jamya laughed to herself because Sahara didn't know how correct that statement was. "Thank you for saving me tonight Jamya. Myself and Alana are both grateful for you."

"No problem Sahara."

Jamya and Sahara collected their personals and locked the gallery for the night. Jamya sat in her car and checked her messages. She'd gotten text messages from Emerick and Jalyssa. She opened Emerick's text first, *"Thank you for a night filled with beauty. Beautiful art and a beautiful woman."* Jamya blushed and responded with, *"You are very welcome. I enjoyed our time as well."* Then she read Jalyssa's text message. It said that she, Diamond, and Sapphire were going to Club Night Life and to meet them there. *Club Night Life. That's where I know Emerick from!* Jamya texted Jalyssa back that she was on her way. That plan was quickly squashed by Jalyssa's response, *"Shit got real at the club. Come by the girls' apartment."*

"Oh shit," Jamya said before she pulled off.

When Jamya got to Diamond and Sapphire's apartment, the girls had started on their third bottle of wine.

"What's going on y'all?" Jamya asked with her eyes focused on a puffy eyed Sapphire.

"Well..." Jalyssa started when Diamond and Sapphire didn't say anything. "We went to Night Life. We did our usual; VIP, drinks, and party. It was all good. Then the DJ gave a shout out to Mark for his engagement."

"What?"

"Exactly! Needless to say it didn't go well after that."

After the incident at Night Life between Sapphire and

Savannah, she and Mark continued their "arrangement". As far as Sapphire was concerned she was still the main woman in Mark's life so she was pissed off to find out she wasn't.

"You okay girl?" Jamya asked Sapphire.

"Other than feeling stupid, I'm good."

"Well we know you're not stupid so that's not even a concern."

"I believed that sorry motherfucker when he said he was in Vegas for business but he was there getting engaged," she spat and guzzled down the wine in her glass. "He was so slick he even spoke to me while he was there. Sorry bastard!" she added between drunken tears.

Jamya, Jalyssa, and Diamond comforted Sapphire until she finally passed out on the couch. Once Jamya and Jalyssa got to their apartment Jalyssa filled Jamya in on the scene Sapphire caused at the club before leaving.

CHAPTER 14
Surprise Surprise

Mary Ann waited in the sitting room for Emerick to come home from the art gallery. She sat smugly, happy with herself and her ability to handle her family's business. Amyra brought Mary Ann some tea and Emerick got home shortly after.

"Hello Mother," he said when he saw her, "What are you still doing up?"

"I was waiting on you darling. Come sit and tell me about the show."

"It was actually nice. There were some really great pieces there."

Jamya being the best of the pieces, he thought with a slight smirk on his face.

"Good. Did you pick anything good up for the office?"

"I purchased three paintings and one sculpture," Emerick said proudly.

"Sounds like a success to me. I can't wait to see your selections."

"They will be delivered on Tuesday."

"Splendid. Anything exciting take place?"

"No not really."

"Hmmm," Mary Ann said softly.

"What is that look for Mother?"

"Nothing my dear."

"That is not your nothing face."

"It's just not the response I was looking for."

"And what response were you looking for Mother?"

"That possibly you met someone."

By that time Emerick had a suspicious look on his face. He knew his mother was up to something and after her latest shenanigans with the Shaniece situation he knew there was no telling what that something was. Reluctantly Emerick asked, "What are you up to Mother?"

"Whatever do you mean?"

"Don't insult my intelligence. What did you do Mother?"

"First off, do not take that tone with me SON. The reason I asked you to go to the showcase versus allowing you to send your assistant was because of Sahara's assistant. She is a beautiful and smart young lady; with a clean background I must add. I think she would be a good fit for your wife."

"What!?!" Emerick exclaimed shaking his head. "Just when I think you can't outdo yourself, you do."

"I was just trying to help Emerick."

"I am a grown man and I don't need your help finding a wife."

"Do not bring that grown man crap to me because you have not used sound judgment very often Mr. Grown Man."

Emerick had grown angry and stood up from his seat, "I'm not going to do this with you Mother."

"Yes you will! Sit down Emerick. You will not run from this conversation like you run from everything else."

Emerick sat, "I do not want to argue with you Mother, but I am no longer a boy."

"Your actions say otherwise. You are the heir to a multimillion dollar industry and you're sleeping with any bimbo who is giving it up. As if that is not bad enough you have a child flapping in the wind."

"What-"

"Do not try it Emerick. I know about the child." Emerick sat in shock, showing no emotion in his face. "What did you think that I would give you almost a hundred thousand dollars without checking behind you? You are not that good of a liar Emerick. I followed the money to Ms. Jade Swanson. Imagine my surprise when I found out she was pregnant; with your child. So again I say your sound judgment in your personal life is not the best. Lucky for us all that does not stand true with your business sense."

Emerick sat there defeated on the inside. Mary Ann let him know that she expected him to date Jamya and make her his wife. He sat and listened as she went on about her vision for his life. Emerick liked Jamya and felt a connection but he did not like the pressure from his mother. Though Mary Ann's tactics were bananas, she was right in her assessment of his sound judgment.

****

"Pops can you meet me for lunch?" Emerick asked Allen over the phone.

"Of course son. Where do you want to meet?"

"At the country club at noon."

"See you then."

Emerick and Allen's relationship still remained slightly strained, but his father was the only person who could understand his situation.

"Excuse me Mr. Jeffries, Mr. Adjei is here to see you," his secretary Maria said over the intercom.

"Thank you Maria. Send him in."

The door opened and a tall, slender, cocoa brown, South African man entered Emerick's office. Emerick got up and greeted him, "Louis how's it going buddy?"

"Very well I must say," he responded with a defined African accent.

"How was your trip?"

"One of great profit."

"I like to hear that. Have a seat." Louis sat at Emerick's meeting table. "Would you like a drink?" Emerick asked as he walked to a bar area.

"Sure. A Vodka straight up."

Emerick made Louis' drink and himself a Vodka Tonic. "Now on to business," he said placing the drinks on the table.

Louis placed a briefcase on the table. He opened it and pulled out a velvet bag. He poured the contents in the top flap of the briefcase showcasing over twenty carats of diamonds that ranged in sizes.

"Beautiful Louis."

"Aren't they? But the guys also found something unique," Louis said as he pulled another velvet bag from a compartment.

The bag contained one single diamond that he handed to Emerick. Emerick's eyes lit up from the uniquely colored diamond.

"This is beautiful. Let me get my loupe and scale." Louis sat with a pleased look on his face as Emerick got his things from his desk drawer. Emerick sat back down and looked at the diamond through the loupe. "This aquamarine tint to it is exquisite." Louis nodded his head. "Oh, and then the pink ice shine it gets once the light hits it." Emerick placed the diamond on the scale, "One point four carats. Lovely. This was a great discovery. Is there more?"

"My cousin has the guys searching the location where this one was found."

"Good job my friend. Please keep me posted." Louis gave a head nod. "When will you returned to Sierra Leone?"

"That is something I wanted to discuss with you. Though this trip was good as far as the goods; it is getting harder to extract the diamonds. The security is tightening. I placed them on my person to get them through. If I was to get searched then we would have a problem. I will have to go to the drawing board and bring some solutions."

"No problem. Here is your payment," Emerick said handing Louis an envelope.

"Thank you old friend. Until next time."

Old friend was the correct term. Louis' father was Emerick's grandfather's "blood diamond" connect in Sierra Leone. He used the money he'd made through their illegal dealings to move his family to the United States. Emerick and Louis met once that happened. They played together as well as learned the business from their prospective sides. Emerick and Louis shook hands and Louis left.

****

Allen was seated at the table waiting when Emerick arrived at the restaurant. Allen was happy that Emerick reached out to him so he did not want to be late. He was lonely since Mary Ann issued him divorce papers and attempted to take everything he knew away.

Allen lit up when he saw Emerick, "Looking good son," he said and greeted him with a hug.

"Wish I could say the same," Emerick said looking at his father. Allen was unshaven, eyes were droopy, and though he was dressed nicely his clothes were wrinkled. "You alright Pops?"

"Not really but I made my own bed. How's your mother?"

"She's her. She's actually why I asked you here."

"Oh my. What has she done now?"

Emerick's response was delayed by the waitress that came to their table. "Good afternoon gentleman. I'm Penny and I will be your waitress this afternoon. Can I start you off with a drink?"

"I'll have a martini," Allen said.

"And I'll have a Vodka and Cranberry and a cup of water."

"I'd like a cup of water as well please," Allen added.

"Okay. Would you like to start with an appetizer?"

"Actually yes. The Shrimp cocktail," Emerick replied.

"Alright. I will put that order in and be back with your

drinks."

When Penny walked away Emerick and Allen continued their conversation. "So what did your mother do THIS time?"

"She has selected a wife for me."

"What?" Allen said sitting back in his chair. "I might need to tell Penny to bring me two drinks for this."

"She says my judgment isn't always the best, which isn't a lie," Emerick said thinking about Jade and what he did to her. "I met the woman and really liked her, but I instantly grew resentment toward her when I found out I was forced to be involved with her. Then I cannot figure out if she is in cahoots with Mother. She told me to marry her or forfeit my birth right in the company. Mother has really gone off her rockers."

"Son she's been off her rockers," Allen said with a chuckle. "I took the bulk of the abuse. Now the focus is solely on you. What are you going to do?"

"I want to say fuck it and let her know I am not a child anymore but you know Diamont Brut is in my blood; it's my life."

"You said you liked the woman before your mother showed her hand so could there be something with her?"

"I don't know Pops. Every time I find myself enjoying

her company I think of Mother's shit."

"Listen Emerick. I was with your mother for thirty years and learned a few things along the way. First thing, your mother is a rattle snake so you cannot take her head on. Second, she controls the checkbook. The last that I recently learned is that she is conniving. Unfortunately you will not win going against her, so make it work for you. What does the young lady look like?"

"She's bad Pops. Beautiful, smart, and real cool."

"Well my advice is make her your wife and get your inheritance. Take this like you would any business deal."

Emerick gave his father a smile. *I wonder if that's how he handled the relationship with Mother. Even after the divorce he's set for life.* The two of them enjoyed their lunch together. Emerick didn't realize until then how much he missed having his father around. That day he buried the Shaniece situation and moved forward.

CHAPTER 15
The Road To Happiness

Savannah found herself getting overwhelmed by the wedding plans and she needed her girl. "Em do you have class today?" she asked through the phone.

"I only had one class today and it was at eight. Why? What's going on?"

"I need some relaxation. Do you want to go to Kiko's Day Spa with me?"

"It depends?"

"On what?"

"If you're paying or not big baller!"

"Ha Ha! Bring your ass."

"Okay. I'll be by your house in a few."

Savannah put aside her notebook, laptop, wedding magazines, and got herself together for the much needed escape from reality. Mark called Savannah as she put on lip gloss.

"Hey babe. How are you?" she asked.

"I'm good. Missing you though. How are you?"

"Stressed out."

"Why are you stressed out baby?"

"Because I'm planning a wedding pretty much by myself while working part time and flying here and there doing modeling gigs."

"Baby I don't want you over there stressed out. You know you could always quit your job and modeling."

"Babe don't start with that again. I don't want you to be taking care of me. We're not even married yet."

"I'm just saying that can alleviate a lot of your stress."

"Or we can scratch this huge ass wedding babe."

"Absolutely not. I want any and everybody to be talking about our wedding." Savannah let out a sigh and he asked, "What's wrong baby?"

"I hear you babe but honestly I don't care about all of that. As long as our closest family and friends are there I'm fine. I know going big is how it goes in LA but the size of the wedding does not matter to me."

"Okay baby I'm sorry. I'm so used to throwing huge parties that I haven't taken your feelings into consideration. Whatever you want."

"Really?"

"Yes," he quickly added, "Within budget of course." Savannah laughed because she could not see herself going over the one hundred thousand dollar budget that he'd given her. "Since we're compromising, is there any way we can speed up getting married? There will be less planning now. So what do you say?"

"Alright but let's be realistic on when because we still need to do bookings, checking availabilities, and so on.

Emily knocked on the door at that moment.

"Babe hold on that's Em."

"I'll go ahead and let you go. We can come up with a date later. I love you sweetheart."

"I love you too."

"About time your ass come to the door," Emily stated when Savannah came to the door.

"Yadda yadda. Get your butt in here and hush up. I was on the phone with Mark."

"Of course," Emily said rolling her eyes.

"What?" Savannah asked with her head tilted.

"Nothing."

Savannah looked at Emily again, "What Em?"

"It's just that you've become one of the girls we talk about. EVERYTHING is Mark, Mark, and Mark."

Savannah put her hands to her face and said, "Oh my goodness Em you're right. Next thing I know I'll be barefoot and pregnant breaking my neck to have his dinner on the table."

"I don't know about all of that, but yeah," Emily said with a laugh. "Don't worry about it, Emily is here to save the day. Let's go. We have some massages waiting and you better be paying."

****

"Girl, this shit's like a fairy tale! It feels too good to be true."

"Hope it's not really too good to be true," Jalyssa mumbled as Jamya went on about the few weeks she and Emerick had been dating.

"Did you say something Lyssa?"

"No. Something was caught in my throat."

"Oh okay. Are you alright?"

"Yes. Go ahead I'm listening.

"Yeah girl. We're going to have dinner on his family's yacht. A yacht Lyssa! I've never even been on a regular boat before."

"You've hit the jackpot with this one Mya. Word on the street and internet is that he's worth millions! You got a great payday at your fingertips. Just stay focused and don't be falling in love and shit."

"Of course."

The truth was Jamya wasn't focused at all. She'd gotten caught up in the time and attention that Emerick had been giving her. The gifts were nice as well but as far as Jamya was concerned she liked him even without the extras. Jamya was falling for Emerick fast and hard.

CHAPTER 16
The Nuptials

"I must be crazy getting married so fast. What was I thinking?" Savannah panicked.

"Calm down babes. It's just butterflies. Yes, you did pull this wedding out your ass, but you love Mark and that's all that matters," Emily said comforting Savannah. "Shit, the way you pulled this wedding together I'd think your ass was pregnant," she added with a side-eyed glance. Savannah took a deep breath. "Bitch you better not be!" Emily exclaimed.

"Hell no! My ass is just trying to breath and not pass out."

"Oh. I was about to say! We don't need that."

"We..."

"Yes we. You know I'll be your baby daddy!"

"You're so silly!" Savannah said with a laugh. "I'm glad you're here Em."

Here was the destination wedding in St. Thomas. With Mark insisting they speed up their wedding, Savannah booked a Caribbean cruise with their closest family and friends. The wedding was to be held on the beach of the Ritz-Carlton, where Savannah and Mark would honeymoon after everyone else departed on the cruise ship.

Savannah put on the borrowed Sapphire earrings. Her reflection in the mirror eased some of her tension. The wedding coordinator knocked on the door before entering, "Are you ready Ms. Biggs?" She let out a soft gasp when she focused on Savannah, "Oh my you look stunning."

"Thank you," Savannah said with a smile.

"Your father is in the hallway waiting and your husband to be is on the beach waiting. So we are ready when you are."

Savannah took a deep breath and looked at Emily who gave her an reassuring smile. "I'm ready," Savannah confirmed.

Savannah met with the overly excited Royce and they all made their way to the ceremony area. Savannah's butterflies, worries, and anxiety subsided when she saw Mark standing in front of the flowered alter. *This is perfect,* she thought as she made her way to Mark to begin her life as Mrs. Mark Roderick.

****

I can't believe you're really doing this," Jalyssa started looking at the packed boxes, "Especially with a prenup. Bitch you've fell and bumped your fucking head for real."

"Lyssa don't start please. I love him."

"Fuck that shit."

"Uhhhhh…Fuck that shit." Jamya huffed. "Have you really thought this shit out though?"

"I have."

"Okay, so what if this fairy tale shit don't work then what?"

"Then I will have my own money that will be accumulating interest to fall back on."

"Again I say fuck that shit. I don't know what you've done with my 'let's get this money' friend, but I need her back. This 'I'm in love and life's' good bitch is tripping," Jalyssa said.

Jamya laughed but she knew Jalyssa was serious, "Are you done yet?"

Jalyssa rolled her eyes and said, "Yeah I guess."

"Good because I'm my sister's keeper…" she probed.

Jalyssa forced a smile, "…and I got her back."

"Plus that just means I'll have to spend enough while we're married if that's the case."

"Hell yeah!" Jalyssa added with a high five to Jamya.

"Now let's go get fabulous for my special day."

****

"Emerick everything is going as planned," Mary Ann said referring to the wedding she'd pretty much single handedly planned with some input from Jamya to be held on the grounds of their estate.

"That's good mother," Emerick said with no enthusiasm what-so-ever. "Has Pops made it here yet?" he added in an attempt to rush her out of his room.

"No your father is not here yet," she said smugly. "I'll be sure to send him your way when he gets here. I have to meet with the caterer now," she said as she exited.

"Bruh, your mother is stoked about this wedding," Mike added once Mary Ann left.

"Yeah."

"She's more excited than you are. You good bruh?"

Emerick hadn't told Mike about his mother's plots and threats. "Yeah man. I think I'm just getting cold feet. You know your boy never thought about giving up his pimp card."

"Yeah I know, but I think you got a good one. You know me and her girl used to fuck around and I ain't never heard no bullshit about her so that's good. Plus she fine so you'll be good. No disrespect."

Emerick smiled, "She is fine as hell though." *Definitely not the worst person to be stuck with for a few years. Here I come trust fund.*

****

Jalyssa, Jamya, and Jamya's mother and sisters all looked around the Jeffries' guest house in amazement.

"Shi-, shoot their guest house is bigger than most people's REAL house," Jalyssa said. All Jamya could do was shake her head because Jalyssa was right. The Jeffries' guest house had four bedrooms, four and a half bathrooms, two living spaces, a game room, and a pool.

"Wow" and "Wo" came from Jasmine and Jessie.

"You're really marrying into some money aren't you?" Cynthia whispered to Jamya. "This place is really something else. Now I know why this big ass rock on your finger was nothing for him," she said showcasing the ring made with the unique colored diamond that Louis gave Emerick.

There was a knock at the door and Mary Ann walked in along with Amyra. "Hello everyone. Welcome," she said walking towards the gang. "I am Mary Ann. You must be Jamya's mother."

"Yes ma'am," Jamya interjected. "This is my mother Cynthia and these are my sisters Jasmine and Jessie. And you already met Jalyssa."

Mary Ann greeted Cynthia with a hug, "You have an exquisite daughter. I'm excited to welcome her into our family."

"Yes, she is quite amazing," Cynthia agreed.

"This is Amyra she is here to help you all in your preparation for the ceremony. Any questions about the house she can help with that as well."

"Thank you very much for your hospitality Ms. Mary

Ann," Jamya said.

Mary Ann smiled, "I'm off to speak to the cater. I was on my way there when I heard you all had arrived. Make yourselves at home and I will see you shortly." She left and everyone got settled to prepare for the events of the day.

CHAPTER 17
Shit Happens

2 years later...

Savannah stepped out of the bathroom of the hotel suite. She smiled, happy about the reaction she received from her outfit; a teddy, thongs, and pumps.

"You like it daddy?" she asked seductively with a finger in her mouth.

A head nod and a "Hell yeah," confirmed what she had already knew; she had him.

"Show me how much," she said as she approached him. Before she knew it Savannah was tossed on the bed, "I like it when you're rough," she stated.

"Oh yeah," he said with a smack to the ass. "I've been thinking about tasting you all day," he said flipping her over and tugging at her thong.

"It's all yours daddy. Taste it," Savannah purred followed by an "Ahhhh," from his initial suck of her lips. Wetness oozed from Savannah as she enjoyed the pleasurable act.

Fuck this shit feels good. Damn he can eat some pussy. Too bad this will be our last encounter, Savannah thought before she

146

exploded.

"Yes baby that's what I'm talking about," he said as he played with her clit.

"Oh baby," Savannah moaned.

"Play with that thing for me," he said reaching for a condom.

Savannah played with her clit anticipating her final time of feeling him in her walls. Luckily, she didn't have to wait long before he filled her. *Damn, that feels good,* she thought as she got worked around the bed.

Savannah was at her climax when she was instructed, "Say my name."

"Oh baby."

"Say my name," she was told again with quicker thrust.

Savannah never said names to avoid mixing up names but he would not give up. He pounded Savannah until she yelled "Oh Brad!"

"Good girl," he said feeling accomplished. "Oh shit Savannah I'm about to cum." There was a knock at the door at that moment. "Fuck!" he yelled attempting to remain focused and to release himself.

The knock continued with an added, "Housekeeping."

"Come back later," he exclaimed.

"Housekeeping," came from the door again along with a

key card being inserted.

"I fucking said come back later," he yelled still deep inside of Savannah.

"No, I will not come back later," came from an angry woman followed by a camera snap.

"Fuck! Candace what are you doing here?" Brad yelled hopping off of Savannah.

"I would ask you what you are doing here but I already know; fucking off on your wife! Fuck you Bradley! I want a divorce," she said and stormed out.

"Your wife! What the fuck Brad?" Savannah said from the bed covering herself.

"Baby, let me explain."

"Explain your ass out of my room you lying cheating bastard," Savannah said as she collected her things and went into the bathroom. "Don't let the door hit you in the ass on your way out!" she yelled through the bathroom door.

"Fuck," she heard Brad say on the other side of the door.

Savannah cleaned herself up and waited until Brad left out of the room. Once she heard him leave she exited the bathroom and laid across the bed. *Guess I'll stay here tonight since the room is already paid for.* "Thank you Brad," she said feet crossed and relaxed.

There was a knock on the door. Savannah answered the door expecting to see Brad but it was his wife. "Come in Candace," Savannah said moving aside.

"That piece of shit…" she started as she stuck her hand into her purse.

Savannah stood there and watched Candace's hand exit the purse. She pulled out an envelope and handed it to Savannah. "Here is your final payment. Thank you so much."

"You're very welcome Candace. Thank you for trusting Biggs Inc. with such a delicate matter."

They spoke briefly and Candace left out of the room. Savannah got back to her relaxation, but not before she ensured every bit of the ten thousand dollars Candace owed her was there. As she laid there she thought about Mark as she often did after a job.

They'd gotten divorced just six months prior. It was a nasty breakup and she was still a little bitter. Savannah moved to Los Angeles, where she still resided, immediately after their honeymoon. As far as Savannah was concerned everything was fine in their relationship; she loved Mark and Mark loved her.

However, she didn't know about his love for women. In addition to Sapphire, Mark sponsored several other women to carry out the fetish play he was into. Everything hit the fan when one of the side chicks, Monica, stuck a hole in the condom. After confirming that she was indeed pregnant, she quickly made it her business to fill Savannah in on the "good" news. During her investigating Savannah found out about the others. That along with the hefty divorce settlement were her motivation to open Biggs Inc.

Savannah popped a bottle of wine and poured herself a glass. "To you, you sorry piece of shit. May you and your trashy baby mama rot in hell."

CHAPTER 18
Daddy's Home

"Hey Em. How's it going?" Savannah said through the phone.

"I'm good sugar lumps. Just calling to check on you. What are you up to in the big city? Still grabbing those men by the balls?"

"Yeah," Savannah said with a laugh. "My latest victim was Bradley Fisher. Sexy as hell, rich, and no damn good! Not only did he have his wife sign a prenup, he had his lawyer add a bullshit one sided clause to further screw his wife. But the soon to be senator wouldn't dare try her with the evidence she's collected."

"Y'all and y'all rich people problems. Glad I'm broke as shit."

"Yeah okay…" Savannah said with another laugh. "All in all things are good. I'm on my way to the gym now."

"Okay now. Keep it right. Keep it tight."

"Got to. Are you still coming to visit?"

"Well…" Emily started.

"Well nothing Em, this is the third trip we attempted."

"You know I'm scared of flying."

"I don't know why but-"

"You don't know why? Try because they crash."

"Then get your ass on the train or the bus, but a plane would be quicker. I really want you to come visit me. Even if I have to fly down to fly back with you."

Emily let out a defeated huff, "Okay…but your ass better hold my hand if I need it."

"Of course I will," Savannah said with a huge smile on her face.

"I hope them LA boys ready for all this lusciousness."

"Girl you're a mess!"

"Just saying. Well go get your workout on and I'll talk to you later."

"Okay Em. Love you."

"Love you too."

Savannah grabbed her gym bag and went into the gym.

****

Jamya was content with her life and what she and Emerick had built together. Outside of their home, Emerick bought Art of Art for Jamya, as well as some outreach projects that Jamya spearheaded. They were truly a power couple in everyone's eyes.

"Good morning baby," Jamya said to Emerick with a

kiss.

"Good morning," he replied as he tied his tie in the mirror.

"Let me get that for you," Jamya said.

"Thanks. What do you have planned for today?"

"I'm going to hit the gym this morning, check on the gallery, and then either do some shopping or go to the spa. Do you have a busy day today?"

"Yes, I have a meeting with the board first thing this morning and then I'm conferencing with potential carriers the majority of the day."

"Well you definitely look good enough to handle all of that," she said as she put the finishing touches on his tie.

"Thanks," he said with a smirk.

"Do you have time for breakfast?"

"No, I'll grab something at the office."

"Alright. You have a good day honey." Jamya sent Emerick off with a kiss and they both started their day.

Jamya spotted Savannah on a treadmill when she entered the cardio area of the gym. Their paths had crossed several times after their initial club encounter, to include hers and Mark's wedding party and Mark's re-grand opening of Night Life.

Jamya went to the treadmill beside Savannah, "Good

morning."

"Good morning," Savannah replied looking up at Jamya.

"I didn't know you went here. Savannah right?"

"Yes," she responded cautiously.

She knew Jamya and Sapphire were friends so she treaded lightly, not knowing the motive behind the pleasantry. The actuality was that since Jamya and Emerick got married she hardly spoke or hung out with Diamond or Sapphire.

Jamya sensed her hesitation and added, "I'm sorry to hear about you and Mark. I don't condone Sapphire's actions. You've always came across as a nice woman and you, hell no one for that matter, deserves to go through something like that," in attempts to ease her mind.

"Thanks."

"No problem," Jamya said as she got on the treadmill.

They finished their treadmill session without exchanging any more words. They met back up in the locker room. *Damn, I'm hungry,* Jamya thought.

"Hey Savannah would you like to grab some breakfast?"

Savannah being the out spoken person she was said, "What's your angle? We've never so much as had a real conversation since the night we first met. Now you talking like we're best friends."

"Honestly, it's just good to see a familiar face. My life

has become pretty boring since Emerick and I got married. Outside of Jalyssa and I getting together once a month or so, all I see is my staff and people who are busy kissing my ass. I didn't mean anything by the invite. I promise I don't have a hidden agenda."

Savannah sympathized with Jamya because she too felt the same way after she moved to LA. She agreed to go to breakfast with Jamya.

****

"Hey baby," Emerick said.

"Yeah whatever," Jade said.

"Don't be like that. I know I'm late but I'm here," Emerick said with a forehead kiss.

"Yeah, I guess your highness needed you this morning. I don't know how much longer I can take this Emerick. Your children and I need you."

Emerick took a deep breath and looked at the sad faced Jade, who stood wearing a round six month pregnant belly. After Mary Ann brought Emerick's misjudgments and wrong doing to the forefront, he reached out to Jade. He pleaded for months for her forgiveness. She eventually forgave him and they developed a cordial relationship.

After six months of feeling out Emerick and the situation, Jade allowed him to meet their daughter Lyric. Lyric awakened a love inside of him that he never imagined existed. He found himself wanting to be around her as often as he possibly could with a new wife and an inspector gadget mother.

Jade and Emerick's relationship escalated when he took her and Lyric on a business trip he took to San Francisco. Though they started with an agreement, Jade had become restless with their almost two years and a baby on the way situation.

"I am and will be here for you and my children. Especially with little Bryson on the way because a boy needs his father. I cleared my schedule for you so you have me all day. Now fix your face."

"Daddy. Daddy," Lyric yelled as she ran in the room.

"Hey daddy's angel," he replied as Lyric jumped in his arms.

"I missed you Daddy."

"I missed you too baby girl."

Emerick felt like a big dog because he had the best of both worlds.

CHAPTER 19
Challenge Accepted

"So you and this chick are friends now?" Jalyssa ranted when Jamya told her that Savannah was joining them for lunch.

"Don't be like that," Jamya replied.

"I'm just saying. It went from y'all workouts and breakfast to shopping and now ME sharing MY best friend today."

"Oh...so you're jealous?"

"No I am not. That bitch don't have nothing on me. Thank you very much."

"Good because NO ONE could ever take your place with your crazy ass. Now let's go eat."

"You're lucky I'm hungry cause the only reason you have time is because your beloved is out of town on business," Jalyssa stated with rolled eyes.

"Lyssa now you know that is not true."

"Yeah okay."

Savannah was seated on a bench outside of Olive Garden when they pulled up.

"Hey girl. Looking good," Jamya said looking at Savannah in her tangerine and navy striped romper and gold strappy wedge heels. "I'm sure you remember big mouth Jalyssa."

"Ha ha very funny," Jalyssa said.

"Yes, I do. Nice to see you again Jalyssa," Savannah said with a smirk. Though Savannah had been skeptical of Jamya at first, she enjoyed the level their relationship had grown. "I'm starving."

"Me too," Jalyssa added.

At least they have their greediness as a common ground, Jamya thought with an added smile.

"What you all smiley for?" Jalyssa questioned.

"Oh, nothing. I'm hungry too."

The ladies' lunch was going well when Jamya received a call on her cell phone.

"Mrs. Jeffries. Hello this is Maria," Emerick's secretary said.

"Hello Maria. Is everything okay?"

"Yes. I know Mr. Jeffries said not to interrupt this weekend, but I need to verify the address for the crib delivery."

"Crib delivery?"

"Yes, for your friend Jade," Maria said hesitantly.

"Oh yes Jade. Emerick must have been trying to do it as a surprise. He's so thoughtful," Jamya said trying to contain her surprise.

"Oh okay. The information I have is Jade Swanson, 1724 McDuff Avenue. Is that correct?"

"Hold on Maria, let me get a piece of paper to write that down. I'm sorry. I'm a visual person so things register to me better when it's in front of me," Jamya said as she grabbed a notebook and pen from her purse.

"Oh I totally understand Mrs. Jeffries. Let me know when you are ready."

"Okay…I'm ready."

She heard Maria shuffle papers before she repeated, "Jade Swanson at 1724 McDuff Avenue."

"Yes, that is correct. When are they delivering this crib? I'd hate to say something prematurely."

"This afternoon between three and five."

"Great. Thank you Maria," she said pleasantly.

"Thank you Mrs. Jeffries and I hope that you and Mr. Jeffries enjoy your weekend. I hope I didn't interrupt."

"No you didn't," Jamya said as her body temperature rose.

Jamya hung up the phone and immediately Jalyssa was on her. "What's wrong Mya? Who the fuck is Jade?" Jalyssa asked hoping it wasn't another "new" friend.

Savannah took a more soft approach because she'd seen the look on Jamya's face too many times in her line of work. "What's wrong dear?"

Jamya took a deep breath before she spoke, "This mother fucker has a crib being delivered to some bitch named Jade."

"Who?" Savannah inquired though she had a feeling she was talking about Emerick.

"Emerick."

"That slimy bitch ass mother fucker," Jalyssa said loud enough for the couple at the table next to them to stare.

"Excuse my friend," Savannah said to them. "What?" she said as she turned back to Jamya.

"But wait, it gets better. This business trip he is on is bogus because his secretary thought we were away together this weekend."

"Sorry piece of shit," Savannah whispered under her breath.

"Damn Mya. I'm sorry," Jalyssa said looking at the hurt in her friend's eyes.

"I can't believe this shit." Jamya attempted to hold it together as her eyes began to burn from the tears.

Savannah handed her a napkin and said, "I'll get the

check and we can leave. It's going to be alright Jamya."

"Mya please don't cry mama," Jalyssa said as she took the napkin from Jamya and wiped the few tears that had fallen from her eyes. "Let's go to the bathroom."

Once in the restroom Jamya let go of the tears she had been fighting to hold in. "Come here mama," Jalyssa said with her arms open. "It's going to be alright." Savannah walked in while Jamya's head was buried in Jalyssa's shoulder.

Jalyssa gave Jamya about five minutes to let out her tears before she told her, "I know you're hurting but now it's time to get into defense mode mama."

"She's right Jamya," Savannah added.

Jamya lifted her head but didn't say anything. "You know I got your back." Jalyssa reassured Jamya. "What do you want to do?"

"Honestly Lyssa I don't know." She'd never felt so deeply for anyone and was defeated by her emotions at that time. "My heart hurts so much right now."

"I have a suggestion," Savannah chimed in. "How about we go to Ms. Jade's address and check things out?"

"Then what?" Jamya said sadly with the fear of what she might see when she got there. "Knock on the door and look like the fool I've been?"

"No, we go and observe. Then from there you let me

help you." Jamya and Jalyssa both looked at her crazy. "Just trust me. Wipe your face my beautiful friend. He'll get his," Savannah added matter-a-factly.

"Shit I don't know what you got in mind but it sounds like a plan to me. Let's do it!" Jalyssa exclaimed.

Though Jamya was in a sad place, she could not help but let out a soft laugh at the way Jalyssa and Savannah was ready to go to war for her.

****

Savannah opened her center console of her Range Rover and offered Jamya and Jalyssa a snack while they were staked out near Jade's house.

Jalyssa responded to the offer with, "Nah, I'm good."

"No, thank you," Jamya said.

"Either you're just greedy as hell or you've done this a time or two," Jalyssa added.

Savannah laughed, "Actually I do this quite often. I'm not a stalker or anything though," she added when Jamya and Jalyssa both gave her a side eye. "I'm a certified private investigator and I do surveillance from time to time for my business."

"Bitch what are you a spy?" Jalyssa spit at her.

"Don't mind her," Jamya said waving her hand in Jalyssa's direction. "I thought you had a consulting firm?"

"Yes, I am a consultant. However my consultations are not of a conventional manner. I consult woman who have been done wrong by their significant other on how to get out of their situation as a winner and not the loser they otherwise could be."

"Well damn," Jalyssa said slapping her thigh.

Savannah was engaging Jamya's curious mind when the delivery truck pulled into Jade's driveway.

"Hey the truck's here," Jalyssa said as she tapped Jamya on the shoulder. They watched as Jade came to the door. "Shit. She's big as shit pregnant," Jalyssa pointed out.

Jamya sat with mixed emotions because there still wasn't anything that pointed to Emerick's infidelity; other than his lie about his business trip. The three of them sat in silence as they observed the movement that was happening at Jade's home.

During their time of observation Lyric's school bus pulled up in front of the house. Emerick came out of the house and met her. Jamya watched heartbroken as Lyric jumped into Emerick's arms.

"That bastard has a whole fucking family over here. Oh so you think you can play me? Challenge accepted!" Jamya said angrily. "Savannah you're hired. Let's get this motherfucker."

CHAPTER 20
Move In Silence

When Jamya, Savannah, and Jalyssa left Jade's home that day she went into defense mode. As far as she was concerned Emerick had made a fool of her and the vows they exchanged.

Though she was hurt, the street in her would not let her play the victim. The ladies went to Jamya's home and devised their plan of action.

"Alright baby girl, what exactly are you wanting to walk away with from this marriage?" Savannah asked.

"His balls in my hand," Jamya said in a mischievous tone.

"Okay…other than his balls what else do you want? Money? Cars? Is the gallery in your name? His name? Or both of your names?"

"Shit! She needs all that!" Jalyssa spat.

"Right," Jamya cosigned. "The gallery was a gift. I believe only my name is on it but I'll check the paperwork.

"Good. Also get me a copy of your prenuptial agreement. Myself and my lawyer will comb through it to check for any shadiness."

"Okay."

Savannah jointed some notes on her paper then said, "From this movement on we are on mission 'get that ass', so any and everything needs to be on point. Jamya you are to act as if nothing is wrong. It will be hard because I know everything inside of you wants to choke the shit out of him. To get the things we need you have to be patient and trust me when I say it will be worth it," Savannah said with her hand on Jamya's.

"Okay."

"Good," Savannah said before she turned to Jalyssa. "Jalyssa your mission is to get back cozy with his friend. Can you handle that?"

"Hell yeah! He gives good head!" Jamya and Savannah both shook their heads at her. "Well he does."

"Alright…" Savannah said holding in a laugh. "When is he supposed to get back from his trip," she added with air quotes.

"Saturday."

"Cool. I'm about to go and get with my people. You try to relax and prepare for this battle."

Jamya nodded her head. Savannah said her goodbyes and left Jamya and Jalyssa to their own conversation.

"So give it to me straight Mya. What are you thinking right now?"

"Honestly, I want revenge. The things that we're plotting on wouldn't even phase him, because he has so much money. I want him to hurt. I want to crush him, like he did me." Jamya paused as tears fell, "I gave him my all Lyssa."

"I know," Jalyssa said comforting her friend. "Guess what?"

"What?"

"I'm my sister's keeper so let's go and have some fun. Call Emerick's pilot and have him gas up the jet and let's go."

"Where are we going," Jamya asked through tears.

"Shit, wherever you want to go. You have too many resources for you to feel trapped."

Jamya smiled and said, "You're right. Let's go to the beach."

"The beach?"

"Yep. Let's go to Hawaii."

"That's what I'm talking about. Let's get you packed then we can swing by my house so I can get packed."

"Or we can say fuck it and I swipe the black card and buy what we need."

"Shhhhhhiiiiit. That works too."

"I am my sister's keeper…"

"…and I got her back."

They hugged and got to their getaway plans.

CHAPTER 21
Hello And Goodbye

Emerick enjoyed the time he and Jade spent together. The weekend he'd freed for his "business" getaway was no different. He was elated when he'd received Jamya's text *"Hey Babe. Jalyssa and I are going to Hawaii for a girl's weekend. I'll be home on Monday. I love you."* He responded back with, *"Sounds fun. Have a good time. Love you too."*

Jade was in her bedroom asleep during that time. Emerick kissed her gently on her forehead. Jade opened her eyes with a smile on her face. "Hey babe. What's up?" she asked with a stretch.

"Well I have some good news."

"I like good news," Jade added.

"Jamya's going out of town so you got me another day."

"That's good," she said dryly.

"What's with the tone? I thought you'd be happy."

"Happy about what? The fact that you're still going to be leaving? Or the fact that regardless of what I'm still your mistress? No, I should be happy that I'm carrying your baby and that BITCH gets it all!"

"Calm down baby," he said when she cringed from a pain. "Are you okay?"

"Yes. It's just Braxton Hicks contractions."

"What's that?"

"It's uterine contractions that come before real labor."

"Like now real labor?" Emerick said hysterically.

"Now you calm down. No, I am not in labor. Little peanut needs to stay put for at least another month. I've been having them throughout my third trimester. I'm fine, but back to you. Don't tell me to calm down. Wifey gets the meal and I get the scraps; a few hours here, a few hours there, a day here, and a day there. I love you but-"

Emerick kissed her before she was able to finish her statement. After a long passionate kiss he said, "Just love me with no buts."

"I'll try," she said.

"Try?" Emerick asked before he undressed Jade and made love to her. He succeeded in hushing her as he did on many other occasions.

****

Jade shook Emerick awake around midnight that night.

"Babe," she whispered.

After several attempts Emerick finally opened his eyes. "What is it?"

"I think I need to go to the hospital."

"What?" he asked as he sat up in the bed. "For what? Isn't it too soon for the baby to come? You're not due until next month," he continued frantically.

"I know, but I woke up wet so I think my water is leaking. Plus my contractions are coming rapidly so have Abigail call my mom to get Lyric. Let's go now!" she said through clinched teeth.

Jade went into the bathroom while Emerick put on his pants and went to Abigail, the maid and soon to be nanny's room. When Emerick got back to the bedroom he found Jade passed out on the floor of the on suite bathroom. He quickly moved to her and panicked when he saw her silk grown was soaked with blood and not amniotic fluid. He attempted to wake her and called 9-1-1 when he wasn't successful. He got a pillow for her head and waited until the responders arrived.

Emerick stood off to the side nervously as the paramedics got Jade ready for transport. He watched as they lifted Jade and moved her along to the ambulance. Emerick nervously sat beside Jade in the back of the ambulance. He felt some relief when she came to in the ambulance, but her consciousness was brief. His mind tried to process the things that were said around him but it was all jumbled together; c-section, heart rate, and baby. His confusion and fear gave him the feeling as if the air was being sucked out of him.

By the time they'd gotten to the hospital he was at the beginning stage of a panic attack. Jade was rushed to the operating room for an emergency c-section and Emerick was being checked out in the hall. A nurse checked his vitals; he was given a clean bill of health. Afterwards he fought to gain access into the operating room. He stood in the hallway upset because his attempts were unsuccessful.

Finally the operating physician, Dr. Voss came out. "How is she doc?" he immediately asked.

"I regret having to inform you that your wife did not make it."

"What?" he cried out."What about the baby?"

Doctor Voss paused and Emerick already knew he was going to tell him that his baby did not make it either. It was as if time stopped at that moment. Emerick sat on the floor in shock. He did not hear anything the doctor said about the baby being in distress in the womb and not surviving the c-section. After sitting there in silence, Emerick mustered up, "Let me see them."

The doctor used his professional training to guide Emerick through his decision, but he got pissed off when the doctor asked if he was sure he wanted to see them.

"What the fuck do you mean do I want to see them? Are

you fucking serious now?"

"I apologize Mr. Jeffries, I didn't mean any disrespect. It's just a routine question. Follow me."

He followed the doctor to the operating room. Emerick hesitated at the door. He stood directly in front of the door, unbuttoned the first two buttons on his shirt, and took a deep breath before he stepped inside. His red eyes focused in on a lonely table in the middle of the room. It was as if a spotlight had been shining on the table that held Jade and baby Bryson's bodies.

His steps became short and choppy as he followed Dr. Voss. A tear dropped as Dr. Voss pulled the sheet back. Emerick broke down when the sheet exposed the lifeless bodies. Bryson was swaddled in a blanket beside Jade. He felt pain like he'd never felt before. "I'm sorry," Emerick repeated as he looked at them.

Dr. Voss left out to give Emerick privacy. He held Bryson and expressed his regret to him, before he kissed him and Jade both goodbye. Emerick wiped his final tear. "Goodbye my beauties," he said before he left out of the room.

CHAPTER 22
Karma's A Bitch

"Now this is how rich people do it," Jalyssa said as Anakoni, a member of their all male service team, fed her strawberries. "I hate that it took Emerick fucking over you for you to start enjoying the lifestyle of a millionaire. Love is cool, but this shit right here is amazing." She was referring to the exclusive five thousand dollar a night beach front hut they were staying in. "I never imagined I could see somewhere like this except in my dreams and you swipe a card and here we are!"

"I must admit it has been fun spending his money. I think I want to go back to that boutique before we leave for some more shopping."

"You know I'm down."

"I know," Jamya said with a chuckle.

They laid out in some lounge chairs that overlooked the water that was their temporary backyard.

Jamya's cell phone rang. "It's Savannah," she said before she answered it; putting it on speaker phone. "Hey Savannah."

"Hey girl. How's the vacation going?"

"Great. You should have come."

"I would have loved to but you know I had to work. Which is why I'm calling."

"Okay."

"Well I had one of my guys sitting on Ms. Jade's house, for pictures or what not that could also be used in your favor. Well, he had a heck of report for me today," she said hesitantly.

"What?"

"He said that an ambulance went to the house around four a.m."

"Oh wow. What happened?"

"Well, apparently Jade went into labor."

"Ain't that about a bitch," Jalyssa said under her breath.

"So you're telling me that their fake ass family has increased by one."

"Not exactly."

"What you mean not exactly?"

"Well, it's been decreased by two."

"Savannah, what the hell are you talking about? You're about to kill our buzz with this riddle me this shit," Jalyssa jumped in with.

"Jade and the baby died."

"Shit," Jalyssa said.

Jamya didn't say anything so Savannah asked, "Did you hear me Jamya?"

"Yes I did. That's not my problem. So what's the next step in our plan?"

"Alrighty then. My plan was going to be to use the schedule you gave me to strategically put myself in his path. With this monkey wrench being thrown in the way. I'm going to focus on the surveillance aspect for now as well as your documentation."

"Okay. Sounds good to me. I trust that you know what you're doing."

"Thank you. I'll let you get back to your vacay."

"Thanks hun."

"Later."

Jamya hung up the phone and laid back on the chair. "Soooooo. Nothing?" Jalyssa asked.

"What do you mean?"

"No words? No reaction? You just found out that your husband has another family a few days ago and now you find out his baby and baby mama are dead and you don't say anything."

"My mama always told me if you don't have nothing nice to say then say nothing at all."

"Bitch please! I've known you damn near your whole life and you've NEVER followed that."

Jamya laughed, "You're right, I haven't. Well, I don't give a fuck about him, her, or their bastard kids."

"Damn, sis that's cold."

"Fuck him! Karma's a bitch! Anakoni, some more wine please."

Jalyssa knew enough about Jamya not to push, so she didn't say anymore about the situation. They sat in silence for a while before Jamya asked Jalyssa, "You wanna stay a few extra days?"

"Sure. I don't have shit going on back home."

Jamya grabbed her phone and texted Emerick, *"Hey baby. I'm sure you're busy in meetings and with appointments, just wanted to let you know that we are having a ball. So much so that we are going to stay a few extra days. Hope that's okay. Love you honey."*

"Bitch," Jamya mumbled as she hit "send".

CHAPTER 23
Suck It Up

Emerick called Mike who took him home. Mike was blown away when Emerick filled him in on the situation. He told him the whole story to include their encounter in college. Mike comforted his friend the best he could, until Emerick told him he wanted to be alone. Once Mike left, Emerick closed himself up in the bedroom. The only movement in the house was the staff.

Emerick didn't bother with his phone once he got home from the hospital. It was day three of Emerick's depression state when Mary Ann went to see about him. She had spoken to Emerick and Jamya's maid who filled her in on him being shut up in the room with limited movement.

"Emerick? What is wrong son?" she asked when she entered the bedroom. "Heavens son, when did you bathe last?" she added when she reached the bed. "I've been trying to reach you. Why have you not returned my phone calls?" Emerick laid there staring at the ceiling as Mary Ann continued, "Where is Jamya? Have you ran her off? Talk to me Emerick. What has happened?"

"STOP MOTHER! I am not up for your shit today!"

Mary Ann stepped back shocked that Emerick addressed her the way he did. "Obviously there is something seriously wrong because I know you would not purposely speak to me in this manner. So I ask again, what is wrong with you?" Emerick went silent again. "I am not leaving until you talk to me. So if you are not looking for long term company, I advise you to start talking."

Emerick let out a defeated huff and sat up in the bed. "Jade and my baby boy died. I do not want nor need your criticism. I know I do not always color in the lines of the picture you draw for me, but I do not care. So there you have it Mother. Now you know what's bothering me, so feel free to leave now."

Mary Ann stood there for a minute processing what Emerick had said. "Alright then. I will not leave until I am ready. Where is Jamya?"

"She's in Hawaii."

"When does she return?"

"I don't know."

"You don't know? Don't you think you should know when YOUR WIFE is due to return while you're over here mourning your whore?"

"Don't you-"

"No. Don't you! Don't you sit up in here playing the victim. Don't you forget you have a wife; a wonderful one I might add. Don't you forget that you are the heir to a million dollar company. Don't you lose focus! I don't know what possessed you to continue a relationship with this young woman but that was not the smartest move. I do not care if you don't like what I'm about to say, but you need to hear it. You need to find out when your wife is getting home and you have that long to mourn and then you need to move past this thing."

"This thing? This thing? How about my family? How about my child and his mother? How about the mother and brother of my daughter? You can be cold Mother."

"Don't get me wrong, I'm sorry that the young lady lost her life, but that is not my concern; you are. I will not allow you to throw your life away behind ignorant decisions. Like I said you have until your wife comes home to mourn. Then you will have to move on. Now, I will leave you to your feelings. I love you son."

"Yeah," he said just above a whisper.

Emerick continued to sulk after Mary Ann left the room. Her words danced in his mind until he fell asleep.

CHAPTER 24
When A Plan Comes Together

Savannah worked vigorously. With Jamya's help she was able to install spyware on Emerick's computer. She sat at her desk scrolling through Emerick's old email looking for incriminating evidence when she came across correspondence from Louis and his cousin Amare. The emails were vague and left Savannah curious of what Emerick had going on. She had a feeling it was illegal diamonds after she dug up the allegations of his grandfather's shadiness.

Savannah smiled as she plotted her next move. She knew that she should not take as much pleasure as she did fucking over men, but she couldn't help it. Emily came to her mind because she made it her business to let Savannah know she thought she'd turned cold after her divorce. In the words of Emily she was a "vindictive bad bitch".

Savannah decided to take a break. She picked up the phone and called Emily, "Hey Em."

"Hey chick! How's it going?"

"It's going. I'm working as usual."

"Oh lord," Emily said with a laugh.

"There you go. This case is a little personal though. Remember Jamya, my friend from the gym?"

"Yeah."

"Well, her husband is my latest victim."

"Damn. I feel sorry for both of them."

"Somebody better feel sorry for him because not only are Jamya and I after him but it seems like karma is as well."

"Why you say that?"

"Okay, so she found out about his affair because of a crib delivery for the mistress. We followed that lead and not only do we see a very pregnant woman but a five or six year old little girl."

"Damn. He had a whole family on old girl," Emily said.

"Exactly. But the reason I said karma is after him is because right after Jamya finds out, he lost that family."

"How? She confronted her and blew up his spot?"

"No, it was a whole lot more tragic than that."

"Tragic?"

"She went into labor and her and the baby died."

"Shit!" Emily exclaimed.

"I know, but get this. I thought about postponing the 'hit' but Jamya had a straight I don't give a fuck reaction to it. You know I'm cold, but even I was like 'damn'. Emerick doesn't know the rage he's uncovered in her. I think that if he was on fire she'd watch him burn."

"Damn," Emily said still shocked about the news of Jade and Bryson's deaths. "Seems like you have your hands full with this one."

"Yeah, but you know I like a challenge."

"I know. Well I was going to tell you I was going to come that way next week, but this case is enough to keep you busy."

"Your ass! You're just trying to get out of flying again."

"No I'm not," Emily sang.

"Yeah okay. I'll let you slide this time, but I really need you to get over this fear you have."

"Yes mom," Emily replied sarcastically.

"Yeah. Yeah. I'm going to go Em, I've gossiped and played with you enough. I have to get back to work. I'll talk to you later lady."

"Okay honey. Be careful out there."

"I will. Love you Em."

"Love you too."

Savannah hung up and got back to combing through Emerick's life. "Hmmm," she said as she looked at the list of events he was scheduled to attend.

CHAPTER 25
Moving On

The outside appearance of the Jeffries' household was of a strong loving power couple. But the reality of it was that they both remained busy not to deal with the other. Jamya devoted the majority of her time to the gallery. She was happy when she saw that the documentation of the property proved that Emerick did purchase it as a gift with only her name listed. Jamya was determined to have it booming with business before she divorced him.

Emerick spent his time burying himself into Diamont Brut. Louis' diamonds were flowing well and the excitement of the money helped him coupe with Jade's death. He tried to stay focused on the large distribution plan he had and nothing much outside of that. The more he fought to not think of anything else, the harder Mike fought to put his mind on things outside of work.

Emerick had given into Mike's persistence and decided to go with him to an annual golf charity event versus cancelling as he did with many other events. Mike always accompanied him because of the ladies that attended.

Emerick had thought he'd been let off the hook since Mike and Jalyssa had become an item. The relationship between Mike and Jalyssa slightly bothered Emerick since he had planned on divorcing Jamya six months after receiving his trust fund; which was in less than a year. The two of them arrived at the golf course and immediately started mingling amongst the crowd.

****

Savannah pulled her Range Rover up to the valet parking booth at the golf course's club house. She gave herself one last once over before she got out. Savannah stepped out of her truck and got the attention of every guy around. Though she took a more conservative approach in a simple sundress and sandals, her boobs sat pretty in the boat cut neckline of the dress. She gave the valet her keys and walked into the club house, feeling like Beyoncé as her flowing blonde curls blew in the wind.

Savannah entered the event area. She spotted Emerick speaking to the event coordinator at the donation table so she made her way to the table and accidentally on purpose bumped into him.

"Oh, I'm sorry," she said innocently.

"It's no problem," Emerick replied with not so much as a glance at her; which was okay with Savannah because she had no intention of making her move there.

Emerick continued with the charity business and shot Savannah a cordial smile as he walked off. Savannah made her contribution at the table and then focused on strategically placing herself in Emerick's view throughout the event.

She ran across several of her modeling fans who'd asked if she thought about getting back in front of the camera. She informed them that though she enjoyed it she made a decision to take on the corporate world. Savannah noticed that Emerick was in ear shot of the conversation. She smiled as she saw his ear lift up letting her know she'd peaked his interest.

CHAPTER 26
Timing Is Everything

"I know she said this would take time, but it's been almost seven months. I know that's your girl but what the fuck Mya?" Jalyssa said from a pedicure chair next to Jamya.

"Chill Lyssa. She's working it."

"How do you know? She's been all hush hush with everything. Her ass can be somewhere with her finger up her ass for all you know." The pedicurist Lin gave Jalyssa a strange look. "I'm sorry," she added.

"She's not. I trust her plus we're meeting after we're done here."

"About fucking time," Jalyssa said under her breath. Jamya decided not to entertain her statement and enjoyed the foot rub she had been getting.

****

Savannah looked over the documents she wanted to show Jamya. During her relationship with Emerick she expected Emerick to be like the other rich womanizers she'd encountered, but she'd found out more than she'd bargained on. She uncovered evidence about his illegal diamonds, a hidden Caribbean bank account, island property, and investments that Jamya didn't know about. Those thing didn't surprise Savannah that much because most of her "hits" had hidden assets, but when she got a copy of the trust fund documents(copied and turned over by one of Mary Ann's not so loyal staff members) she was surprised and angered to see that he'd used Jamya from the beginning. She knew then that she needed to speed things up before the terms were met. She'd kept the majority of her findings a secret up until that point not only to protect Jamya's feelings but also because her plan was accelerating quickly. After Savannah's initial bait session at the golf event, she "accidentally" bumped into Emerick at one of his distributing jewelry stores and again at a bistro he frequented.

"I'm starting to think you're following me," he'd finally said to her.

"It must be fate bringing us together. I'm Liza," she said with a bashful grin.

He'd invited her to sit and eat with him. They talked for over an hour that day. He shared lots about himself, minus his wife, and she'd shared a lot of bullshit with him.

Six months later and they were extremely comfortable with one another. He wooed her the same as he did with Jamya; trips, expensive gifts, and time that he'd stole from

Jamya. She'd planned a Vegas getaway; ironically at the same place Mark proposed to her. That was her way of paying homage to the fucks she gave about him; exactly zero. Savannah finished gathering her things and set out to meet Jamya.

The ladies met at the Los Angeles Yacht Charter. Jamya had rented a yacht for their business meeting to ensure that their plans were not heard nor carried by anyone. Savannah followed Jamya's instructions and met her and Jalyssa on the "Beautiful Butterfly". She was escorted to a lounge area on the top deck.

"Hey Jamya. Hey Jalyssa. How are y'all ladies today?"

"Hey girl. Great," Jamya said.

"Hey I'm straight," Jalyssa added as she sipped a martini.

"Good," Savannah said as she took a seat.

A waiter came and asked if she wanted a drink. She got a sex on the beach. They set sail and talked business over lunch.

"So Jamya we're all set for the end of the month. Are you sure that your mother will not blow the top off of our plan?" Savannah asked.

"I'm sure. My story isn't a complete lie. Mom is having a procedure done, but it's an outpatient thing. I told Emerick that I was planning to surprise her, so he won't mention the trip to her. I've also been dropping little things about the trip so he thinks it's legit. He definitely isn't expecting me to show up during your rendezvous."

"Perfect," Savannah said as she grabbed her bag. "I have the paperwork for you. Are you sure you can trust your lawyer with not leaking your intent to Emerick?"

"Yes. She's my personal lawyer outside of the one we share."

"Good. Just do what we discussed. Slide this in with the charity documents for him to sign. Once your lawyer files the transfer paperwork it will be yours."

Jalyssa let out a laugh, "Y'all hoes sneaky as hell! I love it!"

Savannah and Jamya ignored her and continued.

"Are you set to check into the hotel?"

"Yes. I'll arrive a day before y'all will."

"Don't forget to text me your room number so I can get the key to you. Also make sure you have everything you need so you don't have to leave. We can't risk him seeing you anywhere."

"Got it."

"For the record I want the both of y'all to know that I feel a certain kind of way because I'm not going. I know this is a covert mission and shit but a bitch wants to go to Vegas too. Shit, I've been undercover too with Mike," Jalyssa said.

"Bitch please! You been under Mike's covers and enjoying every minute of it," Jamya interjected.

They all laughed and enjoyed the rest of their yacht experience that was on Emerick's dime.

CHAPTER 27
The Jig's Up

"Maria I am on my way to the airport. I told you I was going to Chicago to be with my wife and mother-in-law, so why have you been blowing up my phone?" Emerick said in an irritated tone. He was determined to spend the weekend with Savannah with no interruptions with Jamya supposedly in Chicago.

"Yes, I know Mr. Jeffries," Maria said nervously, "but Mr. Adjei has been calling here collect for the past thirty minutes."

"Collect?"

"Yes, from a jail."

Damn, he thought. "Well, if he calls back accept the charges. Inform him that I am out of town. From there get the information of where he is being held and then let him know I will send my lawyer. Got it Maria?"

"Yes sir."

"Okay. Send me a message through my PDA once it happens."

"Yes sir," Maria said again before they hung up.

Emerick was shitting bricks from the news. *What went wrong? What did they catch him with? Did he call my name?* Emerick took a deep breath and regained his composer. He and Louis had a long standing understanding of how things would go if he ever got caught.

"Louis knows I got him and his family so I have no worries," he said to himself as he continued to the airport.

CHAPTER 28
Vegas Baby

Savannah and Emerick arrived at the Bellagio via car service.

"This is nice baby. The internet does it no justice," Savannah said as they pulled up.

"It is pretty nice. I'm glad I let you make the plans."

"Me too," she said with a smirk.

They checked in and strolled to their room looking like a happy couple. They barely made it to the room before Emerick was all over Savannah. "Hmmm," she said after a passionate kiss. She let out a grin as Emerick guided her to the wall, put her foot on his raised knee, and lifted her skirt. *Damn, I love the perks of my job,* she thought as he slid her panties to the side.

****

Jamya sat anxious in her room. She was happy to have the plan come to an end, but all of her anger still had not taken the hurt away. She sipped on some wine as she waited for the masseuse to come. Ready for her massage, she quickly jumped up when she heard a soft knock at the door. She opened the door and it was Savannah and not the masseuse.

Savannah quickly slide in through the door, "Hey girl."

"Hey Savannah. How's it going?"

"Good. Here's the key. We're in room 3602. He's unsuspecting of any plans against him so we're good. He thinks I'm at the gift shop now so I can't stay long."

"Okay. I will see you later."

"Yes, later."

The masseuse came shortly after Savannah left the room. Jamya let the masseuse Jasmine, take her to a place of sheer relaxation before she took on one of the hardest things she'd encountered in her life; walking in on her husband making love to her friend.

CHAPTER 29
The Time Has Come

Emerick and Savannah had an eventful Vegas day. They'd went sightseeing, shopping, took in a show, and ended the day with a steak dinner. Savannah genuinely enjoyed the day they shared, but she carried anxiety of the night that was ahead of her. While Emerick paid for dinner she excused herself to the bathroom. While she was in there she called Jamya.

"We're about to leave the restaurant now. We should be back to the hotel in about fifteen minutes. Make sure you're in place."

"Okay."

"Are you sure that you're going to be able to do this?"

"Yes, I'm sure."

"Okay then."

****

Emerick looked at his alerts on his PDA while he waited for Savannah.

"Mr. Adjei is being held at the customs holding office at Cape Town International Airport temporarily and then he will be moved to

their jail. Mr. James has been contacted to provide counsel. I will keep you informed on any changes. Enjoy your trip." Was the message sent by Maria. Emerick had briefly spoke to his lawyer Joseph and he let him know he had everything covered. He blacked out his PDA screen when Savannah came from the bathroom and they left the restaurant.

****

Jamya entered the presidential style suite that Savannah and Emerick had been sharing. She was ready for battle in some jeans, t-shirt, and Timberland boots with her camera strapped across her body. She made her way through the suite to the main bedroom. She stood in front of the king sized bed that sat in front of a wall of mirrors. As she thought of the things that took place in the bed, the reality that her "happily ever after" was over overwhelmed her.

Jamya zoned out for about five minutes like her feet were nailed to the floor. She heard laughter come from outside of the suite and was brought back to her current reality; the reality that her husband fucked over her love for him. Jamya left out of the main bedroom and went into the second bedroom, where she hung out until it was time for her to make her presence known.

****

"Dinner was delicious, but I can't wait to have you for

desert," Emerick said to Savannah. She giggled as they reached their door. She fumbled with the key as they stood there. Emerick stood behind her and kissed her on the back of her neck. "Oh baby. I can't focus when you do that."

"That's the point," he said as he rubbed her nipples.

"Mmm…if you don't stop I'm not going to be able to get the key in for us to get in the room," she said slow and quietly.

Shit. We can do it right here. It's Vegas, Emerick thought.

After fumbling for a few more seconds, Savannah was able to get the door opened; with Emerick attached to her from behind.

Emerick didn't waste any time getting her into the bedroom and undressed her. He laid Savannah on the bed and said, "Play with that pussy for me baby." He undressed as he watched her play in the lake of wetness he helped create. He grew with excitement as he watched Savannah use one hand to massage her clitoris and the other to caress her nipples. *Damn,* he thought as he rushed to get naked as well.

Emerick took his final piece of clothing off and moved to the bed. He kissed Savannah sensually on the lips and then planted kisses from her lips down her body to her vaginal area. He kissed her freshly waxed landing zone before he gave her throbbing clitoris attention. He put Savannah's legs on his shoulders and went to town. The sounds that Savannah were making took him into lala land as he brought her to her orgasmic place.

He heard a faint click during that time but dismissed it until he heard the second click. He raised his head slightly and his eyes caught a glimpse of Jamya in the mirror. He looked back in amazement giving Jamya the perfect photograph.

"Jamya," he said as he jumped up. "Baby."

"Don't-" she said as she snapped several more pictures.

He hopped up and grabbed his boxers as Savannah chimed in. "Baby who is this? And what is she doing here?" she asked as she attempted to cover herself.

"THIS is his wife!"

"Wife," she exclaimed. "You have a fucking wife?"

"Yes, he HAD a wife. You can have his sorry ass!" Jamya said as she turned to the door.

Emerick was on her heel, "Baby no. Wait."

"Fuck you Emerick! Enjoy the rest of your trip and I'll see you in court."

"Baby don't-" Jamya quickly left out of the room, leaving Emerick standing in his underwear looking crazy. He knew he was screwed when the door slammed. Once again he'd gotten caught up in his irrational decision.

CHAPTER 30
The Aftermath

One year later...

Emerick wrapped himself in his Versace blanket and stared up at the ceiling. Life during and after the divorce was hard for him. His and Louis' arrangements were not as air tight as he'd originally thought. He spent thirty days in jail on his illegal diamond trafficking, until he was bonded out by his mother. Those thirty days was Mary Ann's slap on the wrist. Luckily for Emerick Mary Ann's pull went far enough to get him out of his mess.

Unfortunately for Emerick that was the final screw up Mary Ann would take from him and she cut him off. She gave him fifty thousand dollars and sent him on his way to fend for himself. Mary Ann ran Diamont Brut until she appointed someone into the position. That hurt Emerick more than anything because he knew he disappointed his grandfather and tainted his name. To further worsen the situation, Jamya received forty percent of the company along with two cars, a home, and a million dollars in the divorce settlement. He had resentment toward Jamya, but could not blame her because not only did he marry her under false pretense, he also had two major affairs on her.

"Hey bro, how's it going?" Mike asked.

"What's up man? It's going. Just about to get up and get ready for work."

"That's cool. I'll see you later."

Emerick shook his head. He went from a multimillionaire with his own seven bedroom house to an average Joe who slept on his best friend's couch. He couldn't blame anyone but himself and maybe Jamya who cleaned out his hidden account.

****

Jamya sipped on her morning mimosa enjoying the beachfront view from the lounge chair. *I'll never get tired of this view,* she thought as she watched the sun rays that gleamed on the water.

Barbados was where she called home for most of the year. She loved living there and thanked Emerick often for the four bedroom and four and a half bathroom Caribbean home. He was furious at first when she revealed that she was the owner due to him unknowingly signing that document as well as the wire transfer document, but she didn't care about his anger. As far as she was concerned he brought it on himself.

Her cell phone chirped to inform her that she had a message waiting. *"We just boarded. See you in a few hours."* Jamya was excited because Jalyssa was coming to visit for a week of island fun.

Life was good. Jamya was glad that she'd closed the chapter of her life that starred Emerick and was happy with the new chapter she'd entered into.

****

Savannah pulled her hair back into a ponytail in front of the mirror. She looked at her reflection and admired how long and pretty her hair had grown within that year. She put on lip gloss with a smile on her face, content about how things played out after helping Jamya with Emerick.

Jamya was generous with the quarter of a million dollars that she'd given Savannah, but Savannah worked for it. She was behind the anonymous phone call to the South African Customs Union that halted Emerick's illegal diamond import. She was quite proud of her work. So proud of her work that she also got the information to Mary Ann. So while he was in Vegas getting fucked in his personal life he was also getting fucked in his professional life.

Savannah got up from the vanity table and grabbed her phone before going to the balcony. She looked at her phone as she walked. She saw a text from Emily saying that she and Jalyssa had boarded the plane. Emily was still not a big fan of flying but she did well with company. Savannah was ecstatic about her, Jamya, Jalyssa, and Emily's plan to have some Caribbean fun.

She had a smile on her face when she got to the balcony. She watched as Jamya sipped her drink. She hated how Emerick did Jamya but was happy that she was able to help her out of her situation. Savannah kissed Jamya softly on her lips.

Jamya looked up with love in her eyes. "Good morning sweetie," she said.

"Good morning baby," Savannah said as she sat next to Jamya.

"Emily texted me and said they've boarded. I can't wait to tell them that we are engaged."

"I'm so excited," Jamya said looking at her ring. "I love you Savannah."

"I love you more."

Savannah cursed Emerick often for being a dickhead and hurting Jamya but his lost turned out to be her gain. She went from the mistress, to the girlfriend, and now fiancé; so she was winning.

THE END

Check Out These Other Great Books By J. Asmara

WHEN IT RAYNES

WHEN IT RAYNES: CLEAR SKIES

VIRTUALLY CHALLENGED

VIRTUALLY CHALLENGED 2

AND THEN THERE WERE TWO

ALL BOOKS AVAILABLE AT
www.amazon.com/author/jasmara
and
www.authorjasmara.com

Made in the USA
Middletown, DE
01 November 2025

20351934R00119